ISBN:
978-1-906669-01-0

Library of Congress subject heading:
humor.

British Library subject heading:
humour.

Published by LDB Publishing
www.ldbpublishing.com

Cover design by Kathryn Marcellino
www.marcellinodesign.com

Sherlock Holmes

and the

Underpants of Death

Chris Wood

LDB Publishing
Manchester

Contents

This book wouldn't have been written without David Griffith. Blame him.

The Groucho Marx impersonators shot
it out amongst themselves.

Sherlock Holmes and the Underpants of Death

During the many years in which it has been my privilege and honour to report the cases of my celebrated friend, Mr. Sherlock Holmes, I have never known him bettered by any opponent, no matter how clever or well written they may have been.

In his heroic exploits against the underworld, I have known Holmes carry out tests of endurance which would exhaust the stoutest. The case of the museum deaths involved Holmes wearing the same socks for over a fortnight, and to crack the devious mystery of the General's missing armour Holmes went without illustrations for two entire pages; a feat which robbed him of much vital exposure. After that particular incident he had to spend a whole fortnight recovering in the pages of *Victorian Hello!* magazine.

Despite his efforts and considerable, nay unmatched, success in the field of criminal investigation, Holmes is relatively unknown, as befits one of the most modest men in the entire city. He can spend hour after hour unapproached at his club, *The Enigmatic Mind,* despite his best efforts.

On a dark night these sinister and mysterious affairs first entered our lives, like a hideous beast weaving its way through the London mists, waiting to embroil the finest analytical mind of his age.

Holmes had been sitting by the window, a pipe in his hands, the glow warmly reflecting against the grey night we saw through the glass. The agitated figure could scarcely be seen ascending the steps outside our chambers, so great and sinister was the night's fog. I felt a tingle in my bones and the unmistakeable thrill of adventure hung heavy in the evening's atmosphere.

There came a knocking at the door.

Mrs. Hudson could be heard telling somebody that we didn't want any insurance and that Mr. Holmes was off in Hollywood being filmed. However, the lady would have none of it and soon found her way into our presence.

The late night London mists must have made a cruel travelling companion. Yet the young lady who made her way to our rooms so late into the night made no complaint of this when she settled into a chair. Her manner was of one who had been through much, and she stood before us with the imploring expression of one in profound need of assistance.

"You must help me, Mr. Holmes. I am in direst need."

Holmes motioned for her to continue.

"I fear sir, that I must confide in you and you alone. So if your friend would not mind excusing us-"

"Oh, very well," I said rather testily, and got of the bathtub and made for the towel hanging on the door.

With a dramatic utterance she clasped at her head and fell to the floor in a dead faint.

"Not another one," said Holmes as he lay aside the paper with a groan.

"What shall we do?" I queried.

"Stick her in the cupboard with the other unconscious clients."

After a time she came round, and Holmes stopped going through her handbag and I regretfully put down her lipstick.

"Oh Mr. Holmes. Forgive my nerves, but a most jarring incident has befallen me. My fiancé, who has recently arrived on these shores, is in gravest danger. He inherited recently, you see, an enormous and rambling estate on the edge of an appalling dark moor called Edward Heath."

Holmes hiccupped on his pipe and turned to raise an eyebrow at the camera.

"And then a most amazing thing occurred. My mother, Lady Boyd-Peterson, recently had a pair of her, oh excuse me sir, her undergarments stolen."

This last disclosure appeared to perturb her gentility greatly, but Holmes and I are seasoned in the art of grace, and assuaged her blushes by nudging each other and making "Wooooaaaagghh!" noises.

"Lady Boyd-Peterson? Her husband isn't old Algie Boyd-Peterson?" I enquired, my curiosity having got the better of me.

"Indeed my late father was named Algernon, sir. Pray how do you come to be acquainted with his memory?"

"Why, he and I were in the same regiment."

"No, really?"

"Yes, indeed."

"Were you close to my father?"

"Oh yes, inseparable."

I was slightly put out at this, that an old army comrade of mine should not have mentioned me to his daughter, especially one as pretty as this. I played moodily with my rubber duck and made little sniffing noises to myself as Holmes continued the conversation.

"What exactly is the cause of your distress?"

"Well, it is so unusual that I scarcely know how to describe it, sir. There is a disturbance upon my life. I do not know if you are familiar with the Baskerville family, but old Sir Hovis died recently and he left a handsome legacy for his sole heir, Sir Henry, who became my fiancé shortly after he inherited, coincidentally."

Very little of positive information was mentioned, and Holmes's manner became strained, and his politeness in bidding her farewell and booting her in the rear as she rose to leave betrayed his disappointment at not being given a case of the complexity which ever delighted him. His mood was clearly soured, and his manner detached as he asked me various details of the girl's family life.

"Did you know the family well, Watson?"

"Why yes, Holmes. Her father and I used to desert together."

Holmes' eyes grew small and tight with thought, and took the opportunity of scribbling a few quick notes for the old memoirs, taking care to leave a space near the beginning for me to include the eventual conclusion as having been my first instinct on the matter.

"Hand me my violin, Watson."

"Certainly, Holmes," I said, turning my back on the great sleuth as I reached for the instrument, discreetly stamping on it once or twice out of respect for his musical skills before handing it over. Nonchalantly accepting his cracked violin, Holmes played a delightfully splintered tune, so distracted was he by the events of the night that he did not even notice the violin was in four pieces.

As a great music lover, I am used to Holmes' singular violin playing, and in the earlier days of our friendship I could often be seen offering encouragement by striking him on the head whenever he reached for the instrument. Holmes' violin playing is a reflective accompaniment to his thoughts; melodramatic and prone to great gusts of narration.

It is with this particular skill in mind that I have spared no effort in obtaining the finest ear plugs money can buy. I sat behind a newspaper between a pair of these, and wondered how much more I could take of Holmes' moody eccentricity. It was bad enough him keeping his tobacco in a Persian slipper, but of late the habit of keeping his feet in my cigar case had been getting me down.

Undeterred by the barrage of cushions and small arms fire, Holmes played his violin into the dawn, and I spent the time as best I could composing lengthy, heartfelt telegrams to the Samaritans.

The case began in earnest on a wet Wednesday afternoon in Baker Street. Holmes was looking at his case notes, and I was practising my Madonna impression by singing into a hairbrush and dancing in front of the mirror. We were disturbed by an agitated knock at the door. Mrs Hudson was out for the day getting waxed, and as Holmes did not stir from his task, I laid down my hairbrush and headed for the door, first taking off my brassiere, lest our visitor should think I was a Whig.

At the appointed hour the lady's fiancé arrived. A gentleman in fine apparel stood before me, his fine features unruffled by the inclement weather. He was evidently a man of some wealth, and I wondered why he had walked in the rain when surely he had a carriage at his disposal, or else could have his pick of hansom cabs.

"Mr. Holmes," he cried. "I'm at my wit's end!"

Holmes smiled, ticked off another stroke on his scorecard of people at their wits' end, and motioned him to continue.

"My name is Sir Henry Baskerville," said he, and posed for a quick drawing as the illustrator marched in swigging a cup of coffee, took the required pencil impression and the shut the door behind him. After he had left, Holmes and I stopped being grim and determined and our guest put his clothes back on.

"The trouble all started, Mr. Holmes, when-"

"A moment, pray," said Holmes. "Would it not be wiser to take your time and tell your story, and begin where the trouble started?"

Our guest did as directed, and for over an hour Holmes and I listened to his rambling. To omit much strenuous and wandering detail, the upshot of the matter was that Sir Henry's mother-in-law to be, the same Lady Boyd-Peterson as his fiancé mentioned (it took Holmes and I a good half hour and not a few diagrams to connect this), had recently lost a pair of bloomers to a thief.

"Pants, Sir Henry, belonging to your fiancé's mother? Are you sure it was not a shoe, one of a new pair perhaps, belonging to you, which is about to be returned as it is essential to the plot that the thief has a shoe you have worn which carries your scent?"

"No, Mr. Holmes. It was most definitely pants. I'm sure I wouldn't get the two articles confused," said Sir Henry as he crossed his legs, thus snapping the elastic.

Sir Henry's guide in England, a noble old gentleman currently residing at Sir Henry's suite of rooms at the Carlton, was convinced that the family curse was afoot, and was the secret at the cause of Sir Hovis Baskerville's death. This was Sir Henry's uncle, who had recently popped his clogs. There was something about a pair of enormous, ghostly pants which all Baskervilles must fear etc. but I don't recall that too well.

At some considerable length he wound his address to a close, and turn expectantly to the recumbent figure of Holmes, who spoke from beneath the copy of *The Times* which was currently draped over his face.

"This is all very interesting as folk lore, Sir Henry, but how, may I ask, does the humble crime specialist fit into your plans?"

"I would be tremendously grateful, Mr. Holmes, if you would accompany me back to my hotel and satisfy the good doctor that his fears are groundless."

Holmes touched the tips of his fingers together, and closed his eyes.

"It is impossible. I am deeply involved in many cases at the moment, two of which near completion even as we speak, and even an hour is too great a cost. No, sir, what you ask is impossible–"

"I'll give you five quid."

"Of course I'll need expenses."

Our guest produced a postal order, and Holmes ran for his hat and coat.

It was with the thrill of adventure in my heart and the feel of money in my pocket that I sped past Berkeley Square, headed for one of the most fashionable hotels in London. Holmes was wearing his special wealthy client coat, with the large pockets designed to hold any ornaments he may wish to remove for analysis.

We arrived at the great hotel named by our new client. As Sir Henry had gone ahead to attend his ablutions, excusing himself by stating that he could scarcely unzip the snake in a public place, Holmes and I made our own way up the steps and into the lobby.

We stood for some moments waiting at reception, smiling ingratiatingly at all the wealthy people who went past and looking down our noses at the peasants. A porter came along to attend to us after Holmes waved him over.

Sir Henry had given instructions that we were to be made welcome, and we were shown to his suite of rooms. Inside, sat in a fine leather armchair, sat a venerable old man with a full head of starkest white hair. His visage was crumpled as if a fine balloon had been slowly deflated. The size of the lenses in the spectacles on the table besides him stated clearly that such vision as he possessed was immensely poor. Upon realising this, Holmes and I put our tongues out to him, and Holmes made 'grab it' gestures with his buttocks.

The doctor stood to greet us, shaking the hatstand firmly by the umbrella.

"I'm pleased to make your acquaintance, Mr. Holmes. Your reputation has preceded you, sir, a thousandfold!" Holmes was impervious to eulogy, and received the old man's tribute with true modesty by making great show of crossing his legs and giggling.

"....and it will be an honour to tell my grandchildren that I once shook the hand of the country's finest bootmaker."

Before Holmes could reply, Sir Henry entered the room. He greeted us warmly, but from his manner it was evident that he had been greatly disturbed in the time elapsed since he left our rooms.

"Mr Holmes," began Sir Henry, clearly in a state of shock. "I found this garment in my private bathroom not ten minutes ago." He held forward a large, one might almost say unworldly, pair of ladies bloomers, easily three feet wide and the same in length. There was a large yellow stain at the front, and a hideous streak of brown at the back.

"Good heavens," I said. "Are they yours? Best have them laundered, old chap, and privately too. I remember a few fellows in India liked something a little bit unusual under the uniform, and they always got the devil if anyone found out–"

Sir Henry motioned for quiet by sticking two fingers in my direction.

"They are not mine, gentlemen. Nor did I give any instructions for my rooms to be disturbed. The good doctor here has not left the room all day, and he swears he saw no-one enter." The old man looked up and gave his assurance of this, addressing the grandfather clock as he filled his pipe with soil from a plant on the side table.

Sir Henry, thus reassured, spoke again.

"Well, you had better hear the myth, gentlemen, and decide for yourselves if this oddity has any substance." The old doctor in the chair stirred with a certain self-importance, and reached into his coat for an old parchment which I recognised from the BBC props department. The old man cleared his throat and took off his glasses.

"It is the oddest thing," said Sir Henry. "Old Ted here needs the thickest glasses to be able to see even a very little, but his vision is perfect with the naked eye." Holmes narrowed his eyes slightly for a moment, then shook his head and began to listen.

The doctor began:

It was in the sixteen hundred and eighty-fifth year of Our Lord that on the mighty house of Baskerville a great curse did descend.

Of the line of Baskerville a man of considerable evil did walk forth in Sir Homburg, a spitting figure of indecency more wretched than any other man of his age.

Sir Homburg's followers included many dark characters, among them some of the most desperate and depraved men of his time. Never before had so many politicians and children's television presenters met under the same roof.

They were all men of despicably foul character. In each chest beat a degenerate heart. All were heavy drinkers and their karaoke sessions often lasted until the dawn. Such terrors were the meat and drink of Sir Homburg's life, and his reputation among the people of the town was of such infamy that each villager would sooner spend a night alone on the dark and fearful Edward Heath than incur Sir Homburg's wrath.

Upstairs was a poor young maid from the village, who had been dragged back to Baskerville Hall by Sir Homburg and his evil followers. She would doubtless have been scared half out of her wits by the language they used, and had not Sir Homburg promised to pay her well for services rendered, nudge nudge, then she would surely have fainted clean away. Sobbing heartily at her fate, she counted the money twice and called medieval room service.

At great length the revels downstairs wound to a close as Sir Homburg finally won at Trivial Pursuit. Thus invigorated, he decided to head upstairs and have a bit of fun with the village maiden. But as he arrived at her room, a huge lascivious grin wiped across his features, his gaze was met with emptiness, as the maiden had somehow managed to escape with her virtue, a towelling robe and one of those expensive trouser presses.

"Bah. And I paid in advance as well!" Sir Homburg's savage temper had been terribly aroused by the escape of the evening's crumpet. He demanded action, and set about it himself before any other man could stir.

The doors were opened, and through the slamming and reopening shutters the men could see a midnight of *severity as the trees rocked back and froth under heavy crashes of wind.*

But Sir Homburg was not a man to be dissuaded, and with a foul oath he called to his stable boy to release the hounds and prepare his horse.

Such was the severity of the night that although they were all men of seasoned evil, none wanted to follow their leader into the darkness and venture onto Edward Heath at such an hour. Their manner was awed, and a unknown horror stirred among the atmosphere of the house; but in spite of this they decided to set after their leader, albeit at a distance.

And so the revellers all followed Sir Homburg out onto the moor. He had stormed far ahead of the throng on his great horse, a pack of savage hunting dogs baying at his feet.

Deeper into the moor the revellers went, their steps grown timid at sudden silence on this darkest and stormiest of nights.

As they approached a particularly dark element of the moor, the remnants of the pack of dogs ran in terror, Sir Homburg's finest hunting dogs cowed and sniffling, their proud nature reduced to naught by the spectacle which lay ahead.

When the bravest of them reached the spot where Sir Homburg had apprehended the young maid, a sight of terror fit to freeze their bowels met their hushed gaze. Sir Homburg and the unfortunate village girl lay dead, with no marks of violence on either of their persons, but it was not the scene of human corpses which filled their veins with ice.

Above the body of Sir Homburg danced a ghostly pair of bloomers, too big to fit any human buttock. They emitted a foul light and boogied with most improper relish cor blimey.

Sir Homburg's face was frozen in death, and wore an expression of complete surprise.

The guests all turned and fled, their spirits all broken by this supernatural hosiery. One of them died in his bed that night of what he had seen, and the rest of them lived out their days as broken men.

To this day, all of Sir Homburg's ancestors have lived in fear of the Pants of the Baskervilles, who will strike again when one of the cursed line be about, at night, when the powers of evil are exalted.

He finished reciting and looked up at us from his parchment, anxious to see what reaction we would have to his tale of dread. I nudged Holmes awake and we met our host's eye.

"Well, Mr Holmes?"

"Eh? Erm, yes well, five and six an hour, ten shillings on Sundays."

"I mean, the myth."

"Ah, well, that is rot. I have no time for superstition."

At these words Sir Henry produced his wallet and started examining it closely.

"And yet the case may present fascinating angles. I first heard of these matters, Sir Henry, through your fiancé. I feel it appropriate that I pay her a visit and see what I can get."

Sir Henry blushed and clasped his fists together. The ferocity of his temperament showed us most clearly that the hot blood of the Baskervilles was not absent in this, the most recent progeny of their line.

"My Elsie is an innocent, charming woman, and moreover, she has her virtue!"

"You misunderstand," said Holmes, eager to assuage our host's anger. "I'm not going round for any of that–" I coughed loudly and muttered 'bullshit.' Holmes continued. "It is merely that the only crime involved with this unusual case occurred under her roof, and I am eager to examine this matter from the most logical root, namely the first actual stroke in this unusual game."

Sir Henry's cheek's lost their red colour and he appeared anxious to make amends, writing Holmes another three cheques as Holmes muttered "oh no, I couldn't possibly" as he did fast work with the rubber stamp. After a few moments had elapsed Sir Henry's restlessness overtook him and he bade us good day and left the room. Having forgotten about the blind doctor's presence, Holmes forget his customary resolve and began cackling about his luck, and how he would spend months investigating this load of old knickers and then retire.

"Don't be so eager to dismiss, Mr. Holmes," uttered the frail old doctor, now near blind once more having replaced his glasses with the words "that's better" as he fell over the cat.

Having had his myth dismissed, the old doctor appeared anxious to leave the room. He made his way for the bathroom, stepping with the confident haste of a man who has memorised the interior of his surroundings. Holmes and I winked at each and silently lifted the man up and set him down in the opposite direction. Keenly oblivious, he wandered further forward and Holmes and I watched as he tipped out of the window with a cry.

We chuckled our way down to the hotel lobby, our step quickened with the thrill of adventure and an eagerness to have lunch. We walked out of the hotel only a few moments later, and I stepped forward to hail a cab as the hotel doorman was struck by a falling doctor.

I made my way through the crowd which had gathered around the stricken two, and held my stethoscope to the top of the doorman's head. I thought for a moment, and delivered my diagnosis.

"You've had a bang on the nut," I concluded. "That'll be forty guineas."

The old man was in more of an anxious state, however, and appeared to be strangling a lamppost, yelling "detect this, you bloody great nit." Holmes and I looked back a moment to see if we could help, and then decided that perhaps our time was better passed elsewhere. We headed for the station, and the start of another thrilling adventure etc.

We settled ourselves in the first class compartment, and rolled our trousers up to the knees and placed school caps on our heads in anticipation of the ticket inspector's visit. After a short time along he came, and once again I marvelled at my companion's ability to transform himself, sucking his thumb and looking upwards with wide, innocent eyes as we were asked for our tickets.

Holmes piped up in a falsetto.

"Two 'alves please, mister."

"That's a very good voice, mister 'olmes, but you still has to pay the proper fare."

"But I'm Sherlock Holmes! Why, just by looking at the marks on your boots I can tell that you own a very large dog."

"That's as may be, mister 'olmes–"

"By your bad regional accent I can tell that you were written in a hurry, probably as the author lost interest in this bit of the episode."

"Sir, I know you're a twat, but you still has to pay for your seat."

My colleague's face showed his irritation.

"Very well. Two third class seats to the scene of the crime, and Watson has a student railcard."

I produced this from my pocket and waved a three year old Glastonbury t-shirt to add verisimilitude.

The ticket inspector consulted his sheets.

"That'll be five shillings please, sir."

"Five shi – you swine! You'll swing for this!"

"Now then, mister 'olmes, there's no need for – "

"Shut it, porky. I haven't got anyone for that murder last Tuesday, and you'll do nicely. Observe, Watson, how closely his eyes are set together."

I agreed, and eventually we beat him down to four and six provided we stood throughout the journey.

The inspector left us, muttering darkly about how fictional detectives never behaved like that in his day. After a brief journey we arrived at the home of Sir Henry's fiancé, which was on the outskirts of Essex. It was a matter of a small cab ride from the station to the address we had been given, but Holmes had yet to ascertain his expenses and so we swiped a couple of pushbikes from outside the railings and peddled our way.

Holmes' thoroughness was legend, and inscribed anew on my mind whenever I played some small part in investigations he was engaged upon. We were here because it was possible Lady Boyd-Peterson's missing pants had been the ones seen wandering the moors late at night, a ghostly howl emerging from its crack, and an unholy brown and yellow light emitting from it.

We rung the bell at her mansion, and a butler appeared and opened the door.

"We don't want anything, thank you, sirs."

"But we come on business," said my friend masterfully."

"We are fully glazed, I thank you, sir," said the butler, about to close the door.

My friend saw that his identity must be disclosed for us to gain admittance.

"It is I, Sherlock Holmes," and then looked at me with keen anticipation.

"The world's greatest living detective," I added, a little late.

Holmes raised his eyes wearily, and impressed upon the man the importance of our errand. He explained with all his powers of description and inventiveness, and a cheque for sixpence, which he signed 'Herbert Rothschild.' We were shown in, and we made an attempt to be haughty in this grand hall by saying, "coo, look at all them pictures," and other such urbanities.

Our hostess was a most noble personage, a genuine aristocrat and one who, despite this puritan age, never entertained the notion of keeping her bristols under wraps. Upon being ushered into her gracious presence, Holmes and I bowed low for a good eyeful, and the Countess treated us to a wide smile showing the many gaps in her teeth, a tribute to her keen interest in political affairs.

We had barely started on the small talk when, from the floors above, we heard furniture breaking. Holmes and I looked up in great astonishment.

"Don't mind that, Mr. Holmes. My Elsie *will* insist on joining this modern fad for exercise. But enough of this. We are about to sit down for lunch, perhaps you could call back later –"

At this point Holmes started rubbing his stomach with an expression of keen anxiety, and I fainted through lack of nutrition.

"....well, of course if you haven't dined yet –" she resumed, and Holmes and I swiftly recovered with a cry of "wahey!" and raced each other to the dining room.

Elsie rumbled down the stairs, breaking several of them as she did so. The butler showed her into the dining room, affecting surprise as he found Holmes and I stuffing bread rolls into our pockets and hiding ornaments about our persons, as if this wasn't done in the best houses.

After a time our visitor from the week before entered the room, and noted our presence with approval, pinching her nose between forefinger and thumb, looking for explanation to her mother, who shrugged and raised her eyes heavenward.

Holmes and I greeted her in a manner befitting professional gentlemen, and the butler brought in the luncheon just as she finished slapping our faces.

It is healthy for the young to enjoy keen appetite, and I well remember the meals I enjoyed as a boy, which my sister enjoyed still more. After watching her leave table, I often marvelled at how such a lithe figure could contain so many potatoes.

I was reminded of this when our hostess's daughter, a fine looking lump of a girl, moved toward the table crossing the room, casting it into darkness. The young lady gave a delightful curtsy, and then joined us. Holmes watched with interest and pointed at her with his trousers.

Her knife and fork became a blur, and she continued eating until the animal noises stopped, whereat the maid came in to wipe down the walls. At this the young lady remembered a pressing engagement and left the room, making a departing statement to effect that she was "leaving the wankers to it." I looked around, and trust that my eyesight is accurate, but I could see no gentlemen who could be described as such, for only myself and Holmes were present.

I was momentarily ruffled, and sat huffily in silence, too hurt even to pocket any of the silver. My companion, on the other hand, is a seasoned professional who does not allow personal feelings or inclinations to interfere with his ruthless pursuit of the truth. Pausing only to ignore a far reaching belch, Holmes began with his questions.

"I should like to address a rather delicate matter, madam, with your permission."

"By all means, Mr. Holmes. If there is any foul play afoot with Sir Henry, then why yes of course I should be most anxious to help."

"I am afraid that I must speak plainly. Although it was your daughter who first introduced me to this remarkable affair, I feel that it is you rather than she whom I must address about this matter."

"You baffle me, Mr. Holmes."

"The Pants! The spectre which has haunted Sir Henry's people since one of his ancestors first made a mess on the moor. The family have been ever since haunted by a ghostly pair of knickers."

16

"And this spectre was in the form of *what*, exactly?"

At which point Holmes displayed his impatience with those who tried to fool his great perception.

"Bloomers, Madam. You know – " he winked and gestured. "Those which hold your husband's delight, eh?" Here he winked again, and made a movement which was an unusual mix of rowing with both hands whilst thrusting the hips in a singular fashion.

I have never, in all my years of association with Holmes, seen him punched to the floor by a lady of mature years. I thought it best not to interfere, and stuffed a handkerchief into my mouth lest Holmes should think I was laughing. After some time she finished, and left with a gesture of contempt. Holmes tugged at his deer stalker, which had somehow been pulled over his head during the ordeal, and cocked a dishevelled eyebrow at me.

"It that the gentler sex, Watson?"

"*(snigger)* Yes, Holmes." We saw ourselves out.

In the hansom cab on the way back, Holmes seethed with red anger. I passed the journey quietly, looking out of the window and suppressing the odd giggle. By the time we had returned to Baker Street, Holmes had regained his customary *savoir faire* and wore the Sioux face of insulted professionalism.

"I will have no more part in this vulgar farce," cried Holmes, slamming the carriage door on his trousers and losing them a moment later as the cab sped off with a great tearing noise. Holmes walked back into our rooms with as much hauteur as is possible for one who is covering his red and white spotted shorts with a deerstalker. At least he was able to preserve some dignity, it was a very big hat.

Back in the flat, when Holmes had retrousered himself, we thought over the next development in this puzzling case. Sir Henry had sent word to us that, if it was convenient, he would appreciate our presence at Baskerville Hall. Holmes weighed the request for a while, but when he remembered that Thursday was bailiff day we packed our revolvers, the expenses book and a couple of naughty illustrations should the story prove to be uninteresting.

The journey down to Baskerville Hall was fraught with excitement, as Holmes and I looked out for the ticket inspector with a better plan than before. Holmes sat tightly clutching the push chair while I sneakily puffed at a cigar from behind my dummy. Our thoughts were of the Pants, and the strange possibilities which the mystery might entail.

We had travelled down during the evening. Holmes had not been available for travel until late in the afternoon, owing to having been busy the night before investigating the underside of his table at the Dog and Hammer.

When we reached the station, Holmes hailed a cab. We particularly wished to arrive as innocuously as possible, to avoid attracting unnecessary attention which may hamper our movements as we investigated the stain which the Pants had left.

Baskerville Hall was a rambling, extensive mansion adjourning many sinister acres of dark moor. The exterior was covered in a long ribbon of ivy, from behind which the stones of the hall sat in grey isolation, apart from the fact that they were all together, or something.

We were greeted by the butler, Barrymore, a short fellow with a bald head. He asked if we had any baggage, at which I replied that we were both unemployed. He bent down to pick up our cases and Holmes took the opportunity of booting him in the rear. Rolling his eyes upward, Barrymore made his way into the drawing room to inform Sir Henry his guests had arrived and that jokes had been served.

As it was late in the evening, we sat down to dinner at the hall. Holmes and I changed into our dinner suit, me wearing the jacket and him the trousers. We are of rather disparate build: Holmes standing a lean six feet and myself being a perfect four foot cube, and as such the clothes are rather poor compromise. I duly sat bunched up to the middle and couldn't bend either of my arms through fear of tearing the seams at the back, and Holmes sat with great heaving sags of material on either side, in which he kept his violin and spare quizzical expressions.

There were eight of us sat down to dinner at Sir Henry's table. In addition to our host was a local specialist and his wife, who introduced themselves as keen ramblers. There were three other people, all locals, who introduced themselves as spares "should the plot turn nasty."

The scene could not have been more pleasant, except for the pictures adjourning the walls having eyes which swivelled back forth and that secret passages kept opening and the lights going out and people disappearing. Come to think of it, it was pretty damn depressing.

Holmes led much of the conversation, holding forth on how it is possible to distinguish between over 144 different varieties of tobacco by simply reading the packet, and I held the table spellbound with reminiscences of my days in India. I had just finished recollecting the riveting tale of how had I the shits for two years without even having time to pull my trousers up when a terrible, single howl could be heard.

The conversation stopped. A terrible hush fell upon the room, and the candles dimmed as the chandelier swung violently, casting the room in a bizarre partial darkness which placed a ghostly light upon the face of each of us.

A scrabbling noise could be heard from just outside the window, and a great blustering windy noise swept through the room and made the candles flicker. We turned to each other in wild surmise, and despite our best efforts it was clear that we shared but one and the same thought.

Sir Henry made an effort to ensure that calm triumphed in the room.

"Give the guests some more soup to wear, Barrymore. We'll all catch our deaths."

Suddenly, the table shook and the butler turned pale and dropped the dish holding the potatoes.

"It's the Pants, the Pants!" cried Barrymore, who hitched up his trousers and ran from the room screaming. Holmes remained calm, following his professional instinct to jump on top of the bookshelf screeching at the top of his voice. I saw Sir Henry who, for all his blood and will, had turned a chilled white. I myself remained calm, and sat there moistening the chair.

After several moments the hideous scratching noise dimmed and a snuffling could be heard diminishing into the night. For a brief while I felt an enormous sense of relief, and in every soul one could detect an ease which had been markedly absent a moment before. Not one minute had passed before it transpired that our senses had been too kind in allowing us to relax even for that scant time.

Outside in the distance, a bloodcurdling scream shook the chill of the night, and I remembered that the old doctor, who had acted as Sir Henry's guide in London, had not joined us for dinner, doubting his powers of self control. He was due to take a perambulation around the grounds and I feared the worst may have befallen him.

In such delicate matters, it is essential to ensure that calm and propriety.

"I'll give you 12-8 the old bugger's snuffed it," muttered Holmes as we ran down the steps outside Baskerville Hall to a scene of horror and dread.

There at the front of the house, lay the good doctor, his face a mask of terror. There were no footprints other than his own, and at first examination there was no sign of how he could have met his end. Holmes knelt down where he lay and took his pulse, watch and wallet.

Sir Henry stood his distance, unsure of what to make of the terrible sight. Far off into Edward Heath's dark and unholy distance we could hear a disturbance deep into the night, as if wildlife were being disturbed by something whose heart lay beyond the confines of the natural.

My gaze returned to the unfortunate doctor, and Holmes standing above the bent figure of Sir Henry, massaging his shoulder and soothing him by saying that corpses were extra.

"But are you sure he's gone?" asked our distraught host, hiding his cheque book.

"Oh he's dead all right," said Holmes, trying to extract the deceased's gold teeth with the pliers he carried around for that very purpose. "I need these for analysis – nnnngh, got the bugger."

"What think you, Mr. Holmes?"

"Oh, that's worth at least five bob."

"I mean, what killed him?"

The unfortunate doctor wore an expression of terror that seemed to freeze our very blood. Whatever had caused such a reaction was beyond our imagination, but I was sure that the analytical powers of the great Sherlock Holmes would be more than a match for whatever fiends of earth or beyond were responsible for this deed.

We returned to our dinner, and for the first time I began to realise the full extent of the dark matters we had entered upon. My troubled mind was calmed by my knowledge that Holmes was a man of iron resolution, and should we be in any danger then our return to London would be imminent.

It has been well said that wherever the threat of death by murder reared its ugly head, Sherlock Holmes could be seen departing with a speed that defied the human eye to follow him.

After the meal, with the stirring demonstration of the power of folklore over the vulnerable mind, Holmes and I went for an evening stroll. I had hoped to spent the time discussing matters as they had unfolded to us with my colleague, but he was in quizzical mood and spent the entire perambulation in distracted state. After a time we paused on the edge of Edward Heath, Holmes deep in his own private analysis of these strange events, and me busy with my own thoughts, recounting my days in India.

After a time Holmes started with sudden energy, and gripped my arm tightly.

"And if it squeals, let it go – ow! Holmes, what the devil is the matter?"

I looked at my companion with keen surmise, and found his face a mask of the most rigid concentration, his eyes shiftlessly rooted to one fixed point shortly ahead. Slowly, and as silently as possible, for fear of giving away our position on this dark, undetectable night, we took our stances.

A scrabbling noise heralded the arrival of that which had captured my companion's attention. It appeared out of a bush, a scarcely human figure which snuffled and scratched at the earth. Its lower proportions were covered with mud, and a variety of leaves had adhered themselves to this appalling figure.

Doubtless this terrible sight was once as human as you or I, but was now condemned to wander in darkness, lost forever to the world by poverty. I thought I saw something familiar in the visage, as if a once noble face had been ruined by whatever misfortune tears great and good lives. After an examination of the bushes nearby, which it conducted with a great hissing noise followed by grunts which sounded like "that's better," the apparition disappeared once more into the night.

I kicked Holmes awake from his dead faint and we walked briskly back to the Hall, our nerves not a little shaken by what we had seen.

The next day we arose early, as Sir Henry had expressed a desire to have company whilst he explored the locale. I agreed keenly, but Holmes begged to be excluded as there were many vital clues at the scene of the crime which demanded his attention. Sir Henry had arranged a guide for us, a man called Stapleton who lived on the edge of his estate.

When we left Holmes was mincing around with a magnifying glass held to his eye. We walked for a time, and as Baskerville Hall disappeared behind us I looked back to see him wearing trunks and unfolding a deckchair.

After an invigorating stroll round the back of some railings, where we sampled several drafts of local cider. Sir Henry insisted that we mixed it with white spirit, "to put hair on our chests." I had never encountered that particular cocktail before, and I am sure I would have recalled if I had owing to its unusual effect. From what I can recall, we spent much of the afternoon running back and forth across waste ground pretending to be aeroplanes. It was an odd sensation, knowing that Holmes was hard at work reading the sports page and we were expanding our horizons in such a fashion. Life has its usual moments.

After we had awoken from our refreshing sleep, dusk was creeping across the moor's dank exterior, and it was with hastened if not accurate step that we returned to Baskerville Hall. The doctor's warnings had become poignant in our minds since his untimely death, and our thoughts about the powers of evil being exalted after nightfall spurred us on.

As we returned to the Hall, I came upon a sight which I hoped never to chance across, despite the danger inherent in his profession. Holmes lay face down, dead to the world. There were no visible marks of violence on person, but near his limp and outstretched right hand was a bottle of the variety which hold chemicals.

After a few anxious moments, Holmes revived and answered our solicitations after his health. I asked him if he had been drinking.

"Sorry, Watson, no. It's just that all the labels came off my chemistry set, so I thought I'd test the contents by smelling the bottle. You'll be pleased to hear I've found the chloroform."

With a sigh of consternation at his eccentricity emerging once more, I helped him to his feet.

Our enquires continued the next day.

"That guide of ours yesterday was useful," I volunteered,

"Who was that, the man Stapleton? What is his business with the moor?"

"I could not say," I said, looking perplexed. "Perhaps he has botanical interests, or else he simply needs an encyclopaedic knowledge of the moors for some dastardly crime."

One often says such things without thinking about it.

In Holmes's absence, the Pants had made several other appearances about the village. A nearby farmer, one Arthur Jenkins, swore that he had seen the Pants prowling about the moor at night, accompanied only by the ghastly darkness and appropriate backing music.

The Pants had also been spotted in Tesco's stealing cans of lager, lurking near a primary school in Trent and once appearing on TV to describe its years of psychoanalysis following an unhappy relationship.

Holmes sat with furrowed brow, and our thoughtful solitude was only disturbed by the serving maid who, having noticed Holmes' presence, stormed angrily from the room buttoning up the top buttons of her blouse. Holmes affected not to notice and, to ease the awkward situation I passed him my notes on the case so far, and he perused them for a time.

"Mmm," said Holmes.

"Spell it," I asked, for I like my memoirs to be accurate.

"If I may make one criticism, my dear fellow, it is that in these memoirs you insist on writing, the descriptions are very nearly always inaccurate

"That's not fair, Holmes," I said, going off for a little cry. Holmes, you will remember, is reputed to have been a lean six feet of brain orientated master. In actual truth, Holmes is a pudgy little fellow with bad breath and a tiddler; whereas I am a tall handsome stallion of a man with a wavy mane of hair and manhood like a rolled up carpet. I also have far more crumpet than I ever have time to write about.

We set out moodily for a stroll toward Stapleton's residence, my manner of course not showing any of the bitterness I wore following Holmes' earlier comments. I held my head high, and dragged my feet making little sniffling noises.

"I think this incident may prove an excellent addition to your memoirs, my dear chap."

"Write them yourself, you great ponce," I added indifferently.

"By the way, I didn't mean what I said earlier, Watson," he added nobly. "Your efforts are most appreciated and very effective." With this, Sherlock Holmes grew another foot and lost about two stone. His manner recovered its former élan, and he got chased down the path by screaming teenage girls, who had presumably mistaken him for me.

We arrived outside a stretch of cottages where we had been informed old Sir Hovis's gatekeeper, Stapleton, lived. Holmes walked up to the first cottage and knocked imperiously on the door. There came no answer for some moments, so Holmes knocked again. "God forbid they have met with foul play," he said to me hopefully. After a small time a stirring could be heard within, and the voice of a large male could be heard commenting to the effect that it would be "that bloody great detective."

The door opened, and my colleague introduced himself.

"It is I, Sherlock Holmes," and then gave me a swift kick in the rear as I almost forgot to add-

"The world's greatest living detective," and shrugged as Holmes sent a withering glance in my direction.

The man strained to listen for a moment, and then called back to a frail voice which echoed forward, asking what the bugger was selling this time.

"Here, it's Sherlock 'Olmes, the world's greatest living detective. Do we want anything detecting?"

She replied in the negative, and the man was about to usher us out when Holmes interjected.

"I am not offering my services, sir. Not that you could afford them -" Holmes continued graciously as an old lady, covered in filth as is usual for the poor in these stories, walked forward and grimaced at us.

"No, sir. We are here to put some questions about Mr. Stapleton, who I believe lives nearby, god knows why, you grubby poor person."

The man took a handful of Holmes' shirt and jutted his face forward menacingly.

"Don't touch me," Holmes shrilled. "I don't know where you've been."

The larger man made the unfortunate error of grabbing at Holmes. Holmes, who has made good use of his study of boxing, at once launched into action with a useless effeminate flapping of his hands, accompanied by a chilling battle cry of "you beast you, get off get off get off." The assailant was unharmed by this feeble slapping and proceeded to tweak Holmes mercilessly.

I would normally have joined the throng with glad cry, as my appetite for battle is known and feared far and wide, but I was too busy being chased in circles round the room by the man's vicious grandmother, who sported a nasty looking pair of false choppers. These she held in her hand, and clicked them at my rear like castanets as she pursued me.

I feared for Holmes, and certainly my thoughts at the time were very far away from the dentures of the savage octogenarian who pursued me with such vigour. However I was powerless to help, upon realising this my colleague, never one to let the grass grow under his feet, rapidly changed tactic.

Holmes abandoned the Queensbury rules and kicked his assailant in the plums.

"Aha, never fails, eh Watson?" He looked at me for reassurance but I gave him none. I pointedly blew on my fist and gave Holmes a Meaningful Stare. I wanted him to see that I had felled my own opponent with more honourable means (actually, I had used a club but Holmes had been too busy to notice).

Holmes looked sulky for a moment and ushered aside the waiting cartoonist, who was wanting to get a slow motion still of Holmes in action. I suppose my esteemed colleague did not think that a freeze frame illustration of him booting an opponent in the crown jewels did full justice to the nobility of his career.

We examined the other houses, and Holmes discovered Stapleton's address with a more than usually ungodly display of his detecting ability. He pointed at the nameplate outside one of the houses, which read:

E. Stapleton (killer), provider of luminous things to the gentry and all round shifty character.

"Good god, Holmes!" I said in a voice hushed with awe. "It's, why it is almost the work of the Evil One."

We had arrived at Stapleton's gate just as he walked out of his garden shed, clutching a pot of luminous paint. As we walked, he kicked aside a box labelled "Enormous Paintproof Knickers."

He greeted us fervently, and we shook hands. I noticed Holmes had great difficulty getting the odd phosphorous stains off his hands from where he had touched Mr. Stapleton's palm.

"I wondered if we might interrupt your study for a few moments, Mr. Stapleton, and have a work with you about the terrible occurrences on the moor."

Stapleton inclined his head slightly, as if unsure of whether to speak.

"I have some small theories on the matter, and I wonder if your views match my own." Holmes held up his notebook, the pages of which had spelled doom for a many a villain.

Stapleton ignored him until his guest cleared his throat to speak again. Before Holmes had time to say anything, Stapleton began to address us, in the manner of one who is unloading much.

"Pants? Luminous pants? Why, I've never heard anything so ridiculous. Do you honestly think that I can terrorise the moor by releasing a hideous pair of glowing long johns onto them? I mean, does that sound credible, playing off the incredible dark and eerie atmosphere of this terrible, evocative place and use that as a means with which to dissuade those who would venture forth?"

Holmes looked at him with astonishment, and compared Stapleton's words with the theory in his own notebook, which read "Buggered if I know."

Stapleton wound his comprehensive remarks to a close.

"....why, I've never heard anything so preposterous in my life." said he.

"Hang on, hang on," said Holmes, trying to write the plot down on the back of an old envelope. "What did you say after 'claim the wealth which isn't rightfully mine'?"

"You fool, Holmes. I suppose you think I killed Sir Hovis to get my hands on the Baskerville fortune, owing to the fact that I am the illegitimate heir to the line," he continued, and Holmes, scarcely believing his luck, had run out of envelopes to write on. He was jotting the basis of his case down on the back of a passing servant, which these novels seem to be full of. Doubtless he would give tuppence to the fellow afterwards, having neatly copied out all that he had written on the wretch's grimy person.

"So," Stapleton continued, "I suppose that, you, great detective that you are, immediately noticed that *I* have webbed fingers."

Holmes looked at Stapleton's fingers with bulging eyes.

"And having noticed the Baskerville webbed fingers on the family portraits-"

"What family portraits?" Holmes hissed in my ear.

"So, on returning to Baskerville hall....."

Holmes turned to me with enquiring eyes, "Where's Baskerville Hall?" he began, but I silenced him with a wave of my ear trumpet and continued listening to the plot.

"You realised the validity of my claim to the entire fortune, and think that I will stop at nothing until it is mine."

By this point Holmes had run out of poor people to write on and had started scribbling on his own naked flesh.

And so it went on, evil plans, reviving the old Baskerville legend, knowing Sir Hovis had a bad heart etc. By the time he'd finished, Holmes had given up trying to write the thing down and was lying down, banging his fists on the floor and sobbing.

Stapleton – or our benefactor, as I now thought of him – left with his parting shot :

"Not another word, sir. No, I've nothing left to say," and I for one believed him.

As he went, Holmes lifted his head from the floor and called after him.

"Just a minute," called Holmes after the retreating figure. "Is this the one where I fall off the waterfall at the end?"

Later that evening, Sir Henry demanded a report of Holmes' progress. I was evident that the poor man's nerve was wearing thin, for he kept on referring to my celebrated colleague as "you pompous great tit," and a "waste of good food."

After an uncomfortable dressing down, whereat Sir Henry became so personal I scarce wondered at even my colleague's legendary patience at enduring so intimate an ear bashing, our host left, after having backed Holmes up against the wall.

When he was sure Sir Henry was out of earshot, Holmes shook his fist in the direction he had retreated in.

"There's plenty more where that came from," he muttered quietly. I asked him what his next move was.

"We have no choice, Watson. Sir Henry's patience is wearing thin, and I happen to know he still has cheques left."

"What do you plan to do," I hissed, anxious to discover the exact nature of my masterful friend's scheme with which he intended to resolve this most baffling of cases.

Holmes shrugged. "We'll stake him out on the moor and see what happens. Then one way or another we'll find something out."

"Ah," I noticed my friend's modesty. "You mean, you have worked it all out and must simply obtain the irrefutable proof you need to wrap the matter up perfectly."

"The world's greatest living detective," chorused the Vienna Boys' Choir, who just happened to be passing at that exact moment.

"Don't put it on too thick, Watson. There are no tourists about."

That night we waited for many hours upon the cold, lonely moors. I expect Edward Heath had never that popular before.

Holmes stood by my side, and I could feel his tension as we kept our lonely vigil in a spot so remote that our imaginations took us a merry dance into the horrors that exist only in the night, when the powers of evil are exalted.

"What time is it, Holmes?" I whispered.

Holmes took out his watch and consulted it.

"Half past exalted," he said.

The minutes ticked by at what seemed like enormous length, as is the case when a keen and tense wait is afoot.

At last it seemed our wait was at an end. We could hear footsteps, and Sir Henry wandered into view, fresh from having visited his sick friend. Clearly the visit has taken its toll upon the poor man's already wasted nerves. He could hardly keep his feet in a straight line upon the path as he staggered home, dropping part of his kebab as he did so.

Then it occurred, and I pray the angels and saints that what I saw that night will never be visited upon me or any of my line.

We heard a pounding of hooves, an unnaturally fast, rhythmic pace. No beast could move so deftly along the treacherous moors on so dark a night. My blood curdled even as I stood, and the very moors seemed to shake beneath the vast tread.

It came into view.

Galloping at incredible pace, exactly along Sir Henry's path, was the most enormous, fearsome pair of pants I had ever seen. It was an unnatural green glow along the shadows of the moor's night. Even as my heart stilled Sir Henry turned around, and as he saw that the terrible pants were nearly on him he gave one hoarse cry and fainted dead away.

Holmes raced for the spot where he fell, and I, hand on my revolver, made to follow my friend's bold example.

The Pants could be seen disappearing into the distance. Holmes and I ran after it, stopped twenty paces away, and fired shots after shot at the phantasmic lingerie which had terrorised one of England's noblest families for many centuries.

I had served in India as and army doctor, and was no stranger to firearms, having used them when it came to recovering medical fees from fleeing patients. But Holmes was a crack shot, and emptied his revolver harmlessly into a tree stump four feet away from the hideous spectacle of the Pants.

However, some of our bullets hit home, and the Pants fell and lay still. I stooped to help Holmes attend to the unconscious form of Sir Henry, but I when I saw Holmes had his wallet I decided further medical attention would be unnecessary.

We ran over to the body of the Pants, shining our torches upon the shimmering ghostly bloomers. Wearing them was a wizened old man, clutching at his todger and muttering about economics. I heard several involuntary gasps, and I indeed lost a certain amount of poise as I recognised a man recently elevated to the peerage, who had done sterling work as one of our most recent chancellors.

"It seems that Stapleton, fiend that he was, captured an escaped Conservative peer and kept him in a cage on the moor. Then he would let him roam at night, searching for port and servants, clad in these Pants of the Devil, putting the wind up many of the locals."

"Then surely, that noise at dinner –"

"Yes, Watson. The peer naturally smelt the food and sought it out, with the result that our dinner acted as bait. All over the adjourning village (which we haven't mentioned until now) the legend caught like wild fire thanks to this most cunning exploitation of the inventiveness terror may wreak in the human imagination. Yes, Watson. It was my belief from the first that these unworldly drawers were merely a hoax."

"What, Holmes. Fake Pants! What is this world coming to?"

"I know, Watson. It is the devil's own trick."

"But how is it possible? Stapleton was with the others guests on at least two occasions when the Pants could clearly be seen wandering the moors."

"Yes, Watson. But mark the fiendish cunning. I investigated the scene where the Pants appeared the night we first stayed here. You may remember that I spent a long time examining the spot."

"Well, I don't know about that, Holmes. Certainly I remember hearing that you were wandering around the place sniffing a pair of Lady Baskerville's –"

"Thank you, Watson. Yes, many hours I spent collecting clues," he said, rifling through the sheaf of notes he had taken while Stapleton had thoughtfully dictated the plot.

"It is my belief that the Pants were no more than a human ploy to distract our attention. We must find Stapleton at once and ask him what the ending is."

I clutched my forehead as a most pressing thought alarmed every sense in my head.

"But Holmes! What of the killer? Where is Stapleton,? This ruthless, evil man must be brought to justice!"

Holmes smiled quizzically.

"I think we may confidently leave Stapleton to his fate. He, playing upon the myth of the ghostly bloomers which haunt the Baskervilles, has grown overconfident as to his prowess navigating the moor, and will meet his just desserts very sharply."

As if on cue, a large splash could be heard into the distance on Edward Heath.

"Eeeeaaarrrrrggghhhh...." a voice said, followed by "was that all right, Mr. Holmes?"

Holmes quickly gave a thumbs up in his direction, and then turned back to me, thoughtfully patting a large bulge in his coat shaped like a wodge of cash.

33

"I think, Watson, that that is that."

We returned to the little group surrounding the prostrate intended victim. The recovering Sir Henry attempted to brokenly thank Holmes for saving his life and reason, but Holmes waved him aside, careful to not to miss out on any money.

"Ah yes," he said as we departed the scene. "Never let it be said that whilst evil doers roam free, and while good (and wealthy) citizens live in peril, that the world will be a poorer place owing to the idleness of.....Sherlock Holmes!"

He finished on a definite upbeat, arms akimbo and looking at me expectantly. I looked all around us at a variety of interesting flora and fungi, and yawned elaborately.

"I said.....Sherlock Holmes!" Holmes repeated once more.

"Turned out fine again," I said, and toddled off for a quick slash against a tree.

I turned back to my colleague, who was standing with his recently outstretched arms flagging somewhat and his now departed client nowhere in sight to help.

"Oh, that's rich," said Holmes. "There's bleeding gratitude for you."

I took his arm.

"Let us go, Holmes, and bath. I'll even sit at the end with the taps," and with that Holmes brightened considerably, and we walked off together into our respective dawns.

"and if there's any more of that bloody violin playing ..."

... furthermore, until the bill is paid in full, I will not be drawing any background ...

The Mystery of the Hidden Turd

"One of the most grievous cases of scaredness I ever encountered," announced Holmes over his magnifying glass. In the annals of crime, there is no-one with a more sound understanding of the nefarious, myriad naughtiness deep at the core of the human mind than my celebrated companion.

I walked over to the sideboard and celebrated Holmes some more with a large splash of brandy, commenting as I did so on the unusually generous size of the measure in question.

It was the well known military occasion of the anniversary of the Charge of the Light Brigade, and on this day it is considered bad form for a soldier to be found without a drink. I remembered from my days in India one occasion on St Norbert's Day, on which, traditionally, the bells are rung and the bottles emptied. One of the brigadiers found a second lieutenant sober, and promptly had him shot for desertion of drinking.

Then I remembered I was pissed and asked Holmes what the hell he'd been talking about, as I had regrettably been talking (and writing) bollocks.

"Young Miss Teeson, Watson. A most curious case, intriguing in its very fiendishness. The criminal specialist, as I daresay I may have commented, sees each case as both an entirely individual matter while also being a foreseeable affair that shares numerous strands with different incidents. I do not consider that this little matter will be a disappointment, and I am pleased that it has landed in my lap in the midst of what is, I must say from a detective's point of view, a most lugubrious time. Although I fancy the population of London may disagree with that analysis, eh, Watson?"

"God, Holmes, you do talk a lot of shit," I said, forgetting that, while in the process of enjoying several big drinks, I might forget to edit my comments before voicing them to the great detective.

"Indeed Watson," said he, immersed in his own world. "And yet I feel this matter presents many worthwhile opportunities for the erstwhile specialist. Hand me another magnifying glass, would you?"

I complied and, before long, noises of Holmes' holding one glass before another and peering oddly at things emanated across through my thick drunken haze. Having exhausted my highly entertaining game of shooting the ornaments off the mantelpiece (that last figurine took several rounds and a good deal of careful, one eye closed, tongue sticking out in concentration aiming) I was now somewhat lacking in stimulation.

In the course of a pleasant evening of bottle emptying it is quite possible that Holmes will make certain demands which, on the face of them, might seem perfectly reasonable, yet to the pissed mind, may strike one as impertinence of the vilest order. To prevent this from occurring, I asked Holmes to get the hell on with the plot.

"My client will be arriving shortly. Her problem – a bottom matter, I fear – is causing great distress. It is a matter of a certain delicacy, as she is highly connected at the greatest reaches of our nonsensical hierarchy."

I clutched my brow, forgetting that I was using the hand holding my drink. Wiping brandy off my forehead distractedly, I allowed the monumental news Holmes had just imparted to sink in.

"Great lord! You mean your client is," I tottered and grasped at a chair for support, which promptly collapsed. Picking myself up in as debonair a manner as I could muster, I brushed a thorny splinter from my elbow and stood dramatically about the room. "Royalty," I said, anticlimactically.

"Indeed, my good friend, and nobody knows more than you how much a little grovelling in the right quarter can do for a man's career."

I nodded and refilled my glass.

"No doubt you are correct there, old chum," I informed Holmes with a casual finger stuffed up his nose for emphasis. "Certainly if, by some miracle, you pull this one off, then we need never want for aubergines again."

I pictured a rosy future if this went well. Holmes and I attending court, mixing with the high and mighty, laughing at peasants with the great and the good. I could picture, in my mind's eye, Holmes wearing a great ermine robe with magnifying glass motifs woven into the cloth, and myself in a rather becoming blue ball gown, with my regimental motto written on the back in paint.

I was becoming somewhat ensconced in these pleasing day dreams when a microscope dinked off my head, rousing me from these delightful musings.

"Yes, Holmes," I assured my friend. "Mind focused like a whippet guarding steak. Pray continue."

With a slight repositioning of his pipe, Holmes carried on saying whatever it was he'd been saying before.

"And so, one can only conclude that this, on the one hand trivial crime, is also a deeply unhygienic menace that needs be curbed!"

"Aye," I agreed with the above. "Nobody wants a faceful of shit."

"Indeed, Watson," he said, a faint smile playing about his features like a bee who thought there might be honey up his nose. "I recall your chilling experience with your old regiment, when unseasonable weather blew an entire stack of horseshit directly into your left ear. If I remember the details, you immediately became an ardent devotee of Wagner."

"Indeed so," I said with a shudder, for the incident in question had been one of the strangest of a particularly wild campaign.

The terrible experience occurred on the howling mountains of Nepal, where the winds had loosened many a man's senses. My regiment had been posted there for something under a month when the terrible event occurred.

We had been having rather a nice tea party and an enjoyable game of charades one evening; a regimental tradition which makes it all the rosier when the chaps had to roll out and slaughter the natives the following morning. Being only slightly schooled in the ways of these parts, we circumnavigated any cultural differences by demanding egg and chips at a volume sufficient to pass the language barrier.

Naturally we all believed that our efforts to seamlessly blend into society there had been met with dewy eyed gratitude and approval, but, if that were the case, the feelings were not universal. Our native bearer, a resentful soul, had taken against us; and this despite the fact that we took him under our wing and enslaved him in the hope of making a gentleman out of him once we had finished massacring his family.

This fiendish soul took it upon himself to be the regiment's undoing. Scarcely had we finished the final game of Trivial Pursuit and polished off a last quick one for the road when this serpent began his cunning game.

"I hear the quickest way to the next town is through that valley there, and then up onto the hill by the farm." He pointed the way out to us and, pissed as we were, his excited jabbering carried over our good sense. We made it our way and, soon enough, this devil's plan became clear.

The regiment had been marching scarce an hour when the hideous, much feared Wind of the Rear, as it called in Nepal, took upon us. We covered our noses and waited for all to pass, but alas! our hopes were in vain.

A gigantic mound of camel shit, as stacked by the side of the road, began – almost impossibly – to shift as the wind whipped about its dungy foundations. The air filled with a wretched stench as we continued about our brave, half pissed voyage of genocide. Before we had taken a dozen steps the whole body of men was, to a last limb, engulfed by rancid camel plop.

Our treacherous guide could be heard cackling into the distance; heard, that is, when we had gouged sufficiently at the thick pluglike gatherings of shite in our ears.

To this day, when my delicate nose draws scent of a particularly eggy one, I think back with renewed horror of our terrible exploits in that distant land.

Having been reminiscing for a while, I had rather lost track of what was going on. Looking about me with wild surmise I suddenly discovered a client on the chez longue. From her tear soaked face and general despair, I gathered that Holmes had been playing the violin again.

"Cruel swine," I murmured through clenched lips.

"And then, Mister Holmes, and then – oh, oh!" With that she swooned and, with that being something of a tradition in these stories, I busied myself by telegramming for a pizza. Holmes wafted a bottle of smelling salts under her nose.

She revived sufficiently to regain her poise, and I realised that she was indeed a lady of the utmost refinement and breeding. The tattoo on her left boob was spelt correctly – a rarity among tattooists who service the lower orders, I had learned – and the sovereign rings on her fingers were of finest gold. I made a mental note to remove these for medical purposes should she faint again – the lifting of that much metal being very bad for people of a nervous disposition.

"Naturally you are very concerned that these troublesome happenings do not bother you, of course," cooed Holmes soothingly. Had I any doubt that the lady was, to her nines, minted with cash, then Holmes' pleasant manner was sufficient to dispel any waver.

"Perhaps," continued he, "you should begin your tale again for the benefit of my colleague, Dr Watson. He has been an inestimable assistant in many of my cases, and I should appreciate his bearing on the matter."

"Ah, a problem, eh? I thought I heard you playing *Lust For Life* on your Stradivarius.

Holmes shot me a look that I recognised at once said "mouth = shut," but I ignored it anyway.

The young lady turned to me, and I burped attractively at our guest.

"It began most mysteriously. My husband and I had been holidaying in Dorset, where he has a small holding. We had been obliged to lengthen our stay, due to an unforeseen problem with the servants. Maximillian is a stickler for correctness, and he insisted on thrashing them all before we left."

"Too right," I said. "You don't want to be covered in camel shit." I had been thinking of that filthy swine of a Nepalese, although both Holmes and our guest may not have understand this, for they both gazed upon me with an expression of complete bafflement. "Elementary," I muttered, feeling a berk.

"Anyway," said she at length, eyeing me sideways, "upon our return to London, we found a most foul besmirching of our modest, 84 room Belgravia town house. There was, oh goodness me! far more than a generous dash of dirties soiling our door."

"Dirties?" I jeered. "Dirties? Oh la de dah, forget our arseholes, did we, and leave them to shit upon our dainty, ponce flavoured doorstep? Oo dear, a turd! Goodness me!" And I pinched my nose and began to swan about the room, mock swooning at a variety of seeming offensive items.

"Forgive my colleague, madam," said Holmes with his suavest grovel. "He suffered a terrible injury with one of our eastern campaigns, and part of the shit hasn't been removed from his brains yet." Holmes walked over to me and hissed "Money client! Shut it, porkface!"

42

Suitably ashen faced and bowed, I mumbled a desperate plea for forgiveness, and sat at the lady's feet, sniffing quietly and pawing her knees.

I had scarce begun this most humble endeavour when she stood abruptly. Apparently a most urgent appointment had suddenly made its imprint green upon her memory.

"Oh, I fear I must depart at once. This very second, if not sooner!" said she as Holmes implored her, with his best puppy dog eyes, to stay and write him some lovely cheques.

"You want to make a list of these things, ducks," I advised her. "You could have remembered too late and missed the fucker."

"Quite," she murmured, and left like a bat out of hell.

Holmes sat scratching his chin for a while, looking out of the window at the deep London mist. I surreptiously poured myself a post-balls up snifter and gargled it back. The explosive, prolonged 'ah' which left my lips as the last drop went its merry, purple way appeared to rouse Holmes from his latest reverie.

He peered over at me with ill disguised contempt.

"Far be it from me to dictate your behaviour, Watson, as I know that I myself possess a number of less than appealing habits, but I would be grateful if you could not drive off my wealthier clients and spoil any chance of a lucrative case that comes my way."

I mused for a second on the weight of Holmes' deliberation. Was it true? Had I driven away some of Holmes' paying people? It was an appalling thought. For one thing, Holmes, with his great anti-social way of improving society, would make me pay bitterly. I could be getting screeching violin recitals well into the small hours for months afterwards. Bummer.

"Of course," I began, attempting to lighten the matter, "when she returns, as she surely will, to receive your great wisdom," I grovelled on, "when I'm a little more sober, she will naturally be inclined to pay you even more."

Holmes sucked away at his pipe and gave me a thumbs up.

I relaxed a little at this, hoping that the great detective wouldn't drive me batshit with his constant prima donna behaviour. One or two small courtesies to Holmes and perhaps the whole matter would be forgotten. I devoutly hoped so, and drained another quaff to ease the thought down.

Mrs Hudson entered our sitting room with her usual trepidation.

"A telegram for you, Mr Holmes," she croned, passing my friend a neat square envelope. "And one for you, Doctor," said she, proffering a far larger and bulkier package. I grasped it with alacrity, tore it open and a pizza fell out onto the rug.

"Ha!" cried Holmes, hitting that jarring, near falsetto note he always strikes when a game is afoot. "We have no time for refreshment, Watson, for an emergency requires our attention across town."

I gave up scraping mozzarella from the floor and extracting cat hair from strands of tomato sauce and reached for my hat.

We descended into the fog of Baker Street and Holmes attracted a cab from over the street by shooting out its lamps.

"A trifle rough, Watson, but desperate times call for desperate measures."

"I do so agree," I heartily concurred, discreetly swigging a desperate measure from my army issue half gallon hip flask.

The carriage whisked us across much of murky London's streets and soon we arrived at the scene in question.

"A dastardly crime, Mr Holmes!" cried Lestrade in his lost puppy way as soon as my illustrious colleague strode down the cab steps.

Behind him was a busy crime scene, with plenty of convincing Victorian extras stood about looking aghast behind lots of period detail. A brace of burly constables stood around and twiddled their standard issue huge moustaches.

"So I gathered from your telegram, Inspector," intoned Holmes suavely in his mellifluous tones. I reread the telegram in question, which simply stated "Confused as it gets, for fuck's sake help!"

"Please do state what you know of this appalling matter."

"It was a small hours of the morning matter, Mr Aitch. A hansom cab sped past, with this hand emerging from beyond the velvety curtains, like what the nobs have. The hand was holding a 15 foot pole with a brass knuckle on the end for knocking. The door was answered by the housekeeper, Mrs Twuddocks, and from the safety and shelter of the cab a turd in a jar was hurled in, leaving the housekeeper something of a twitter."

Holmes pondered gravely. I stifled my laughter.

"And how is this unfortunate woman, Mrs Twuddocks?"

"Well, the doctor has stabled her nerves by giving her a prescription for gin."

"Has she recovered her sensibilities at all?"

"It is early days yet, Mr Aitch. Last I saw of her she had the postman in a headlock."

"And you say the carriage was one of the better sort, laid out in rich raiment as befits the easy transportation of one of this city's wealthier inhabitants?"

"She swears so, yes."

"Hmm. That means the assailant must have left one of London's finer districts with a turd in a jar hidden about his person. Most interesting." Holmes paused and allowed himself the briefest of smiles. "Should Watson trifle the reading public sufficiently to publish another tale of my adventures, perhaps he may refer to this as the Mystery of the Fifteen Foot Pole?"

"Some chance, Holmes," I replied, underlining the words 'hidden turd' in my notebook.

Holmes read over my shoulder.

"We must not give in to early theorizing or inappropriate speculation, Watson. It is quite possible this mystery may not be solved so easily. Supposing this gentleman filled the jar while making the journey on his nefarious mission?"

My mind swirled and boggled, a very difficult thing for it to do while pissed off its knackers. Was it possible that a member of our finery was capable of such appalling deviance? Part of me hoped so – it is always very reaffirming when an aristocrat can do anything well, even when it comes to committing dastardly crimes of an inhuman nature. Still, it's an achievement of sorts.

"Are there clues of any kind to be found here, Inspector?" pressed Holmes, eager for information. His face was already showing that boyish glow it always got whenever a truly foul deed had been committed on innocent citizenry.

Lestrade consulted his notebook and chewed a pencil for a while. He seemed to have some trouble reading his handwriting, so Holmes snatched the book from him and, peering closely, was able to decipher Lestrade's child like scrawl.

"There was a statement from the under footman, who arrived some time after, and found the housekeeper in a state of shock."

He snapped his fingers imperiously at a passing constable, who snapped his fingers back and made a 'wanker' gesture at Holmes. Undeterred, my colleague motioned to another policeman for assistance.

"I see from this that the witness often drinks at a nearby hostelry. Watson and I should pay him a visit, and quickly at that, I fancy. Is there anybody you can think of, from the top of your head, who may have committed this outrage, inspector?"

"Well yes I have, now you mention it. I've heard of rebellion everywhere. Single mums, mostly. And foreigns."

Holmes scratched his chin for a while as he mulled this over.

"I am not sure if your intuitions are correct in this matter, Lestrade. I feel we will both be greatly surprised by how this bizarre matter turns out."

Lestrade gave a little gasp and look at my esteemed colleague with awe and wonder.

"Lawks, what goes on in your brain surely is a miracle, Mr Aitch. What gives you that idea?"

Holmes considered for a moment.

"You don't think that shit being thrown about at respectable housekeepers is surprising? Then I am glad I do not live in the same borough of town as you, my good man!"

With that Holmes and I headed off to speak to this under footman in his favourite pub, "The Horse's Dong," which was but a short cab ride away.

We soon alighted from our carriage. Holmes looked about him keenly, and doubtless savoured many fine and revealing clues simply from the smell of oxtail broth that was, inexplicably, hanging in the air (inexplicable, that is, unless someone had been preparing oxtail broth nearby).

Outside the tavern, Holmes gazed for a moment at the rather unsavoury inn sign which certainly lived up to the pub's name.

"I rather think, Watson, that we are in for a rum time of it."

Looking up at the surely exaggerated painting hanging directly above the doorway, I could only agree.

The inside of this public house was a dark, singed and smoky affair. A nauseous mould yellow suffused the walls, and the regulars lugubriously partook of their beverages while saying little, or nothing. It was a typical pub scene for one of these period adaptations of our fair adventures that can be seen on the – not yet invented – television, where Holmes is tall, and dignified (as if!) and I am a fat bastard with the IQ of a peanut.

Immediately we noticed the stricken under footman we had undertaken to speak with. From his gaunt, soured disposition it did not take my colleague's great skills of detection to realise that he had seen a foul day's work, and that it had wrought inner hell about his disposition. He moodily circled his gin and the oily fluid swirled in the glass.

"Good evening. My name is Sherlock Holmes," began my celebrated colleague in his plummy debonair tones. "I wish to speak to you about the recent foulness which befell your employers' home. Have you any details to report?"

A lingering acrid belch was the response, and the man's glazed eyes rolled toward us briefly and his eyes swelled in and out of focus as he attempted, difficult in his sozzled state, to comprehend why we were there. He slowly waved an uncertain finger about for a moment, and then suddenly the light of comprehension could be seen dawning in his face.

"Ah! The shitting!" said he, in the loudest of voices. The inhabitants of the tavern, jaded as they were, barely took notice, although I did notice one of the bar staff blenching visibly.

"So you know of what I speak?" queried Holmes.

"Know? Jesus, it would be hard to miss!" said he. Holmes gestured to the barman for an extra top up. The footman drained this with a single draft and, breaking wind potently into the general midst, toppled over backwards with his eyes rolling up.

"Well, that was useful," I volunteered. "Two more of what he just had," I added to the barman, who was giving the footman's fresh urine stains on the carpet a particularly tough stare.

Due to the inconclusive nature of our visit to the crime scene, Holmes was in a restless state of mind. In the snug of our Baker Street flat he sat pensively, his mind winding out the myriad strands pertaining to the mystery. At length he uncorked himself from his pip and gave speech.

"I beg that you leave me alone, Watson."

"Ah! A three pipe problem, is it?"

"No idea. I just beg that you leave me alone."

Somewhat miffed by Holmes' dismissive manner, I made a big show of how unmoved I was and left the room in a haughty silence, my head held high.

As soon as I was out of the sitting room, I raced over to Holmes' room, where I spent a pleasant hour and a half straining to produce as much shit as possible. I had half filled Holmes' great trunk by the time my cheeks clicked on empty.

I left a trail of toilet paper strewn all over Holmes' possessions, a smirk upon my face and a plentiful array of deep skidmarks all over the furnishings. Lying on my bed for a time I felt a fine glow of satisfaction at a thing well done.

Speculating as to his facial expression when he saw the shit state of his room, I oft gave a rich chuckle. It had been a fine afternoon's work, and I wondered that it had not occurred to me to do so before. Fix Holmes' hash good and proper, it would, so I thought.

I lay in contented silence for a while, blowing off quietly from time to time. I marvelled that my guts had the merest quack left in them after such a thorough emptying. It had been a marvellously satisfying experience, and time after time I relived the glorious experience dump by dump.

Sleep had very nearly claimed me for her own when a disturbing thought shook me back to consciousness. How could I have allowed folly to induce me to act in such a fashion?

49

I was awoken some time later, when the euphonic sound of Holmes' 'rich client' voice filtered through. Resonant tones, dripping with the thrill of the chase were explaining, in thoroughly dramatic tones, of the need to hire a top crime specialist.

Pulling myself with some difficulty to my feet, I trundled into the sitting room. A fine lady, tender in years but bearing a clear weight of grief about her, sat on our *chez lounge*. From her fine apparel, and Holmes' grovelling ministrations, I gathered she had cash up to the nines.

I caught her in mid distress. She was so wrapped up in her tale of woe that she did not notice when I sidled in and pulled up a tumbler.

"My husband received a letter bearing a mysterious crest. Inside it was full of, oh excuse me sirs, excrement."

Holmes was looking keenly at a somewhat soiled envelope in the lady's grasp.

"Poo, you say, madam?"

She gave a delicate sniff - unwise given the subject matter, I felt - and fell back, fortunately in the direction of her chair. Holmes raced nimbly to his feet as she did so and, ever the practical joker, deftly pulled the chair out from beneath her.

His eyes narrowed as he wafted a copy of *The Times* over her face. After some moments the client blinked twice or thrice, took in my presence, and again became the sophisticated lady about town once more.

"I feel so terrible for speaking of such matters in front of gentlemen."

I simpered.

"Most kind of you to say so, madam."

Holmes wrinkled his nose and looked at my somewhat dishevelled appearance.

"Yes, most kind."

"However, I feel that the matter is in the finest possible hands. You will contact me, I beg you, if I can answer any further query."

"Your well being shall be my constant concern, madam," said Holmes in his suavest grovel, and bowed so low I could hear his elastic straining.

Mrs Hudson was summoned to show our plutocratic visitor out, and once again Holmes was his usual high powered investigative self. Some hours later he awoke, and still had not detected the acrid reek of shit emanating from his bedroom.

He busied himself with study of similar misdeeds to the foul ones we were faced with now. Holmes was an expert on crimes involving poo, and the psychology of scatological criminals. He had written a toilet paper which had been published in the pre-eminent Journal of Coprology, published - or should that be flushed? - in Vienna.

For the rest of that day he was a vision of inactivity. The hours ticked by and he scarce moved at all, so intent was his study of the articles before him. I chanced to see, as I passed him by later that afternoon, an object which had so greatly absorbed my celebrated colleague. It was innocent enough when casually glanced at by those unaware of its foul past, but it filled my soul's deepest cavity with a nameless horror; namely dread. Not so nameless, really.

It was the seal of a most notorious gang of criminals who had crossed swords with Holmes on one previous occasion, recounted in a monograph of mine entitled 'The Adventure of The Hidden Cheeks Gang.' Their foul and evil ways were still recollected with gasps of dread horror by even the stoutest; and with a waist circumference of 57 inches, surely I counted as among their number?

The Hidden Cheeks Gang were a bunch of American ruffians who earned a dishonest crust by menacing pillars of society. They mooned their way through

Harlem and the Bronx, turded passing strangers in Washington and on one occasion farted it out with a brigade of Canadian Mounted police, several of whom still haven't regained their sense of smell.

I let out a low, respectful whistle. If these callous gangsters were Holmes' prey in this matter, he would need every ounce of nerve and intellect he could summon. Recognising this was well beyond me, I cracked open a can of mild and started perusing ankles in my naughty postcard collection.

Some time, and many bottles, later, Holmes' consciousness returned to the room from whichever distant layer of his many faceted intellect he had been dealing with. His eyes lost the milky film of vacancy they wore whenever his great mind was truly absorbed.

"Have you a mind for another mystery, Watson?"

I belched supportively and waved a friendly beer in his direction. It doesn't do to skimp on booze when celebrating military holidays. Very bad form.

"Count me in, ducks. We'll get these fiendish shitters and make 'em sorry they dared to turn the air of London darkest brown. Why, I'll see 'em corked myself!"

"Splendid, Watson," purred he with pleased erudition. "I might have known that in you I would find a ready ally. We must not rest until not one Londoner lives in fear of a drive by shitting."

"I take it the fiend has struck again?"

"I fear so, Watson, and this time his dread bottom has aimed even higher up the social ladder. The lady I was consulting with earlier is nothing less than minor royalty, and her position is one of the most delicate, like a gutful of curry seeping its way along the hole's edge."

He does put these things poetically.

"Think you of any reason why this lady's household should be bothered by any such terrible crime?"

"Indeed yes. Her husband had been involved with crack dealing."

Holmes raised an eyebrow quizzically and smiled in his most mysterious way.

"I hardly like to ask, Holmes, but do you mean to imply that her husband was-"

"Indeed, Mr Holmes. He was involved in the pimping of bottoms as hedonistic receptacles."

"Great Scott!" I spluttered, and many more syllables of shock were lost in my moustache.

"So, Watson, my hidden foe is before us once again."

I gasped, tottered and gaped.

"You mean ... Moriarty!"

"No, Watson. The Unnatural Deed is what I mean. The devil's own rumba. For I refer to nothing less than Homosexuality!"

"Balderdash and pshaw," I said scornfully. "It will never enter my head to do the deed with another man, Holmes. Never!"

Holmes' mouth twisted a little into one of his pale, wan smiles. He said nothing but reached close to the ground for several files, his bottom splayed like a turkey ripe for bumming.

"Well my dear fellow, we shall have to face the devil in all his forms."

A bell rang.

"Good lord, Holmes! The telephone has just been invented!"

"Indeed so! Quick, Watson, not a moment is to be lost!"

Racing from our respective armchairs, we intercepted the postman, found the parcel with our new telephone in, ripped open the packaging and answered the phone.

"Hello? Holmes here. Any clues?"

"Mr Holmes, you'd best get down the Yard. There's been another drive by shitting."

Holmes sprang to his feet and grabbed his magnifying glass from its holster. I called into his wake.

"There has been another attack?"

"A particularly nasty one, Watson. We're lucky lives weren't lost. You'd better have a look at the scene of the crime with me. Perhaps your medical experience may prove invaluable!"

Pleased with this proud accolade, I beamed all the way, offending many officers who had been appalled by what they found, and considered my attitude less than appropriate.

Once again Holmes and I found ourselves facing the shocked crowds, vomiting coppers and forlorn, victimised setting of London's stark brick walls. We sidled our way past the press, who were busy invading the privacy of a number of famous people in order to ascertain their view on this most heinous of invasions, and proceeded to survey this madman's work in all its hellish accomplishment.

At once my steely, battle hardened nerves turned to merest confetti. I have seen men with their innards blown out, their outwards blown in and, worst of all, a fine fellow who caught a splinter right in the pork, but the sight that befell my maligned eyes there was without doubt the most ugly deed of which I have ever heard.

The lagoon of excreta threatened to engulf our very clothes with its own vile, odorous niff. A vigorous eastern wind brought lapping waves breaking with brown foam alarmingly close. Several bystanders had clearly been overcome by the stench and one, poor soul, had succumbed to his senses' dearest wish by blacking out but, regrettably, straight into what appeared to be the emptyings of hell's own chamber pot. His twitching corpse lay face down, floating in the bummy mire.

It was far worse even than the time Holmes and I went for a quiet weekend rehinging his stamp collection in Dorset and he blocked the plumbing with a rich, nutty poo; the exact fragrance of which I can still sample, even now.

After inspecting the torrential, syrupy buttock juice which, so great was the spread and volume, threatening to slop about our feet, Holmes turned to Lestrade.

"Aha! A Guinness streamer! I assume you have instigated enquires among the Irish hostelries?"

The good inspector - or the downright crap inspector, truth be told - was at once astounded and dismayed.

"Why no, Mr Holmes, we have not."

"You will note, I trust, the particular gloopy quality of this projection of bottom mud. This naturally invites enquiry as to the diet of the culprit or, more pressingly in this case, the liquid consumption."

"It can't be done so light, Mister Holmes," said the inspector shaking his head. "Loath as I am to throw up any clue into this fear-flavoured, buttocksome matter, I reckons the affair is a trifle more complex than that. 'Tain't just the Guinness as can give a man hurricane arse on a scale so very fearsome; no. Many of the ales in hostelries all over this fair city can turn your insides to stinky mush, sir."

He broke with a lugubrious whine, shaking his head and looking down. Offended by his complicating of the matter, I walked over and tweaked his nose. The inspector was not expecting this response, I daresay, and tried to cover the gaff by hauling open his coat and, from the rack of truncheons nestling within, picked the one marked 'Arse Mangler - this way up.'

"I consider we should leave such trivialities for later, Inspector. At present no person in this locale is safe. And yet what to do - criminal London being the nest of vipers it is, we could be dealing with a vast conspiracy."

There was a sober pause, during which I sang a variety of musical hall numbers. After a time, the inspector, having mused on the matter, spoke hopefully to my celebrated colleague.

"Perhaps we should round up a number of suspects, fill them with booze and do a test firing of their arses at the range in Briddlington? I have contacts in the breweries around here, and a sampling of their most loosening ales could be obtained with little effort. Then we could force our suspects to imbibe a considerable quantity of said beer, have two strapping constables lower their britches and record the results for posterity, in a bucket."

Holmes' eyes narrowed, as they often did when a distinguished member of the Yard was talking crap, as they often did. He mused for a moments and a single note could be heard whistling through his lips; then his nose, eyes, ears, and finally elbows. Holmes had the most musical body when he was at thought.

"We needn't go all the way to Briddlington, inspector. If you see the fine varieties of colour in this puddle of shit here, you will notice a small but very fine trace of ermine lapping at the edges of the pond."

The inspector reeled backwards, a man undone.

"Mr Holmes! I never thought I'd 'ear it said. Not in my lifetime, sir; no, not never!"

Holmes patted him on the bald patch.

"Fear not, inspector. I have high hopes that this sorry, sordid matter will be undone before many more days are out!"

I noticed from Holmes' manner that he was, indeed, bullshitting. Stifling the merest of sniggers, which snowballed into a loud bursting guffaw, I ushered him away.

"Perhaps we should request an interview with one of the finest firearms' experts of our time, who lives nearby, coincidentally."

I staggered, visibly moved. I was amazed that this great man should honour our borough with his presence. His efficiency with a rifle was a byword among military campaigns

Holmes looked at me with an indulgent smile.

"Perhaps it would be wiser if you added to your already considerable alcohol intake at another tavern."

"Great heavens," I cried, "surely the public houses around these parts are not for the likes of I, a humble servant of Her Noble Grace Queen Victoria. Why, they could smell my poverty!"

"Indeed Watson, and see it also, for if I may so opine, there is a growing stain on the front of your trousers."

I peered down at the offending trickle that had indeed grown to a veritable lake on the front of my garments.

"Possibly," he continued, "you should drink less!"

I could see that we were, indeed, opening a can of worms labelled "bollocks."

I said as much to the great sleuth, and he clapped me heartily on the shoulder, said "stout Watson!" as he popped me in the belly with a cheeky index finger. He then produced his magnifying glass and began zooming in and out around my elbow, which was grazed by a Jezel bullet fired at me during an especially patriotic rendering of God Save the Queen at the old barracks in Huddersfield.

I thumped my chest proudly and fell back giggling, and Holmes suggested we should first see one of his lowlier informants, or "poor fuckers," as he is wont to call them in his jocular moods. Before we did so, however, a compromise was reached. We did go to another crime scene, and I had several more drinks, although in cheaper pubs. It was a lot to be faced, if I'm honest, as several victims, too poor and scabby to be mentioned, had indeed drowned in their own shit. Enough to put anyone off colour.

At the corner of one of those cheap sets built in some TV studio we saw Cobblers the Beggar, one of Holmes' best assistants. He smiled broadly when he saw us, baring his three teeth, strangely distorted from years of being poor.

"Ooo Mistah Holmes," he rasped, in his voice which, after decades breathing the sweet air of London's splendid thoroughfares, was reedy and broken.

"Ah, Cobblers," said Holmes, feeling in his pocket. "Here is a shilling" (what do you think he was feeling in his pocket for? Filthy minder reader, with knackers for brains!). "Tell me who comes and goes from Colonel McNab's apartment. Wire me at once if anyone comes past with any large containers marked 'evidence,' 'clues' or 'plot.' Be sure tell nobody of your charge."

With a gracious tap of his imperious nose, Holmes imparted his wisdom and was gone. Realising he was gone and that I had been leaning against the wall and staring at Cobblers for some time gave me a slight start. I turned around and trundled after my taller friend's purposeful strides at a less impressive pace, calling "Holmes, stop you bleeder" at irregular intervals as I puffed along, red faced and sweaty.

Holmes had been heading straight for the domicile of the good Colonel, and rapped on the door. A tall, dome headed butler answered and peered at us.

"May I help you, sir?" was all I could think of to say to this imposing buster, but Holmes elbowed me out of the way.

"I am Sherlock Holmes, and I wish to talk shit with your master."

"I am not surprised, sir. I have heard a great deal about you." With that he showed us into the mainstay of the house, namely the Colonel's sitting room.

There stood the proud warrior of whom I had heard so many admiring accounts. His eyes held the same fierce, steady, bloodshot determination of a man who, if legend is to be believed, once crossed the Khyber Pass dressed as a local woman to avoid paying his bar bill.

Holmes and I were treated to a rare and privileged view of the great warrior's personal collection of military souvenirs. His mighty career was duly represented by relics from a grateful Empire.

There were tusks from the great African elephant, teeth from the savage Rangers supporter and the shrivelled testicles of a tribal chief from Llandudno. In addition to which were a bewildering variety of stuffed animals, reaching from the wild moustache pelicans of Tasmania to the mighty scrotum ants of Timbuktu.

Holmes, who, it should be remembered, was not a military man, stood there with disdain. He smoked in an aloof manner, the way he always did when somebody other than himself was the centre of attention. It always riled him when he could not go through his ridiculous charade of false modesty.

Meanwhile, our gracious, mightily decorated host regaled me with tales of his courage and wisdom. Holmes stifled a yawn and made the 'wanker' sign behind the good Colonel's back. Our fine host, my expressly admired hero, continued.

"Another great tale that I am reminded of, featuring myself in a prominent, noble and exaggeratedly heroic role, took place in the summer of '84. I had been stationed in Cumwallah, a province to the left of Zaire, unless you are holding the map upside down, in which case it is to the right.

"A battalion of the Queen's Own Helmets had been making nobs of themselves among the natives. A terrible rumour had been passing its way around the men, talking of the most heinous and bollock-scratchingly awful case of the clap ever to be heard of by man or beast."

I sat enraptured, drinking in every last nuance of his wondrous tale. The prestige of his noble person kept me in shrunken reverence. In his majestic presence all I could do was gape and tip brandy all over my face as I clumsily tried to drink. Holmes rolled his eyes and filled his pipe. I could tell my jaw had dropped at the part where the Colonel talked of shooting crabs off the nuts of his privates, but I cared not, such was the nerve and derring do involved.

Some goodly length of time passed as the honoured soldier waffled on. I sat like a teenage girl in the presence of a famous actor, giggling and wildly crossing my legs at his merest joke, and Holmes sulked for my neglect of his own talents.

"It was rumoured that the vicious Wahatsu tribe were planning on slaughtering all the British soldiers in the region. One of our native bearers, Assan, told us this when we finished supper one night."

To my intense and lasting regret, I never did hear the end of the tale, for Holmes, apparently losing the will to live, quickly invented a clue.

"Quick Watson, to the carriage!" he yelled, guiding me to the door by my scrotum.

"But Holmes," I protested, when we were out in the street taking a refreshing breath of London's noxious air. "Surely you know of this man? Of his great talent for tickling the natives into action by firing curry powder at them from his blunderbuss? I wish only to worship at his feet," I complained, uttering protestations like a spoiled child being dragged away from a sweet shop.

"Quiet, Watson! Not a moment is to be lost. It is now my belief that the conclusion of this bilious, not to say overflowing, mystery is to be found in the highest quarters of the land. Royalty, Watson, royalty - it is their hand, or rather, arse, that is at the bottom of this, I am convinced."

I mulled this over in my mind as we continued on our way. It really made little sense, even after I reread the above plot device several times more. In fact, it made even less sense then.

We made our way to Buckingham Palace, passing vast swathes of tourists buying tasteless City of London tea towels, mugs with the crown emblazoned upon them, and Prince Alberts.

We rapped on the gates of the palace and explained that we desired an urgent meeting with our Sovereign. Time in the narration being short, we were shown right in.

Holmes and I waited fearfully while our great Queen held court without, doubtless attending to great and mighty affairs of state. We could hear a deep draining noise, followed by a tinkling sound suspiciously reminiscent of empty beer cans being hurled about.

"A weighty matter of state is being considered, of that I have no doubt," I solemnly commented to Holmes. He was on the verge of agreeing with me when a thunderous belch interrupted him.

"Ah yes, a matter about the winds, I don't doubt," was all Holmes could think of to say once the paintings had stopped rattling.

Next to us sat Sir Horace Fiddlington, who made his name by inventing the world's first mode of transport to be powered entirely by spanking bimbos. Upon hearing this, Holmes and I immediately volunteered for duty, but apparently we were not bimbo material. A great loss was how I saw it, but that's his poor judgement, so fuck him.

All along the ermine trimmed waiting room we could see an elaborate display of finest, wealthiest art. A great multitude of portraits adorned the walls, portraying our Gracious and Most Royal Family in a variety of poses.

To our immediate right was a portrait of our Wondrous Sovereign playing darts in India, and to her right was the Most Noble Prince Albert clutching at his trouser parts with a manly tear glistening in each eye, for some eponymous reason. On the other side was a detailed presentation of Her Splendiferous Monarchialness putting the shot in Aberdeen.

On the opposite wall were a variety of still life pictures by the finest royal sycophants; those whose tongues are brownest and whose lips are entirely invisible beneath their thick coating of royal mud. One such piece was a bird's eye view of Cornwall with "The Queen is ace" stencilled into a spider's web.

I admired this without restraint, for its pageantic wizardry quite made me forget the brutal repression I had seen practiced under the Crown banner during my army days. A set of silly values can do wonders to undermine the guilt caused by such campaigning.

I was still admiring this fine canvas, blotting out the flatulence bellowing out of the queen's chambers, when I jolted upright at the bitter memory of the terrible scandal that painting represented.

It was an appalling incident. The picture in question was a heinous piece of bolshie nonsense, with a similar bird's eye view of Cornwall; only in this latter painting the weavings in the web read "The Queen is a silly fat bitch."

The scandal was a most appalling disgrace, from which all but the stoutest reeled in stunned horror. Luckily the culprit was found attempting an even more horrendous act of rebellion, having the words "Vicky R is a bloater" tattooed on his arse, that he may moon the royal carriage to devastating effect.

It was only by a great stroke of good fortune that the tattooist realised that the treasonous inking he was now a party to would see him dancing on the gallows (bizarre how being executed puts some people in the party mood), and so he bravely dobbed the fellow in.

It was dark day for the Empire when this foul-hearted treachery was exposed to the world. All of Great Britain was in shock, although subversive sniggering could be heard echoing far and wide across the Empire. The culprit was publicly flogged, tweaked, twatted and then eventually, in her ever-lasting mercy, our Infinitely Wise and Imperious Majesty, our Gracious Sovereign, had his testicles flattened with a steak tenderiser.

This naturally brought about something of a change in the man. Nowadays he may be found outside "The Queen's Boobies" in Croydon, talking in a loud, high-pitched voice about how great the royal family are. I believe it was he who coined the phrase "they do a bloody difficult job," a statement much beloved by editorials featured in our less broadsheeted press.

Thus do we observe that the most severe physical punishment really doesn't harm the brain at all. Indeed, it was once my pleasure to buy this gentleman a small brandy at "The King's Chopper" in Reigate.

The painting before me on the wall was, however, a rather feeble attempt made by this fellow to amend the wretched horrors he had inflicted upon the world. It had none of the scope or grandeur of his earlier, more rebellious offering; however it was at least fit for gentlemen to stare at.

My attention had been somewhat wholly absorbed by the paintings, and my musings on their rare and curious origins. I failed to notice the statuesque figure stood beside me, and, as such, when he struck the little silver gong he was carrying, he sent me into a foul blue rictus of naughty words.

"... poo, tits, pissbone, flapsmear ..." but I was interrupted by Holmes' nonchalant movement to cut off the air to my profanities with a deft shoe to the pods. I flailed at the air for a moment and went purple.

"Her majesty wishes to know if you are ready to be received into her presence now," intoned the pompous tit of a butler. Holmes immediately went into his best fawning pose, which appear to gratify the retainer. Regrettably all I could do was massage my recently assaulted knackerage, which he may have misinterpreted.

A pair of enormous doors opened with an imperious clatter. With trembling legs we approached the great figure who stood before the throne. She was shorter and podgier than popular portraits may have us believe, but Holmes and I were no less awed.

Queen Victoria has been verified as the fairest of her sex by a great many courtiers from all around the world, and I concur with this. It's just in matters of appearance that she looks like one weird bitch.

She gazed haughtily at us with an expression like a snake digesting a gerbil. Her beady black eyes had the dull lifeless stare of a reptile, and the grey blob of hair woven into a beehive emerging out of the back of her skull looked, oh, charming.

Holmes was about to speak when a strangely arresting scent momentarily stopped his words. From under Her Majesty's skirtage there came the unmistakeable flopping sound of a monarch laying a cable into a jam jar.

Holmes tottered backwards, and, if nothing else, I had out of the affair the rare distinction of seeing my colleague dumbfounded.

"Great Scott!" he whispered, *sotto voce*. "All the turds are of royal lineage! Those stools in captivity must be worth a fortune! I must raid Lestrade's evidence locker forthwith!"

"Mister Holmes, we are pleased to meet you," said the Gracious One, wafting at the air with her hand slightly as she spoke. "Please pay no attention to the odour. As you are of lower class than our royal self, I am confident it comes from you."

"Quite so, Ma'am," said Holmes with a deep grovel.

"I am told you are here regarding the mysteries of certain downright whiffy crimes which have been perpetrated on the streets of our fair capital."

"That is correct, Your Majesty."

"No doubt you saw the clues scattered about Colonel McNab's sitting room. A collection of our royal stools have been adorning his London quarters for some time. We were fearful that scientific analysis would reveal that the shit used in these crimes was of a royal line, and I wished to plant evidence on a scapegoat. McNab was volunteered."

"I understand."

"For you see, it was our royal husband who, I regret to say, has committed these atrocities. He will commit no more. Our royal doctor has made rough and savage use of an outsize cork, and there will be no more of it."

"But why, if I may make so heinously bold as to beg an indulgent answer from your great Majesty, did your other half wish to go hurling royal sewage at the great unwashed of London? What had they done to deserve such blessing?"

Her sovereign madge considered for a moment, and allowed once more that air of royal constipation to cross her battleaxe features.

"These dreadful crimes of bowel vacation, or, as the tabloids fancifully call them, the drive-by shittings, do require some explanation. I will be blunt. My husband, Prince Albert, driven insane by having a spiked piece of metal driven through the end of his cock, has gone insane, for some reason. He was doing them. Blame someone else."

Holmes muttered an awed cough under his breath.

"Surely Colonel McNab has already been volunteered by your regal self for this matter?"

"He was. But I have changed my mind. It is very rare, after all, that one finds a man who is a good enough shot to hit a pubic crab from right off the royal bush."

Both Holmes and I were a little staggered at this, but what the hell. Our Gracious Sovereign was, however, generous enough to allow Holmes to remove several souvenirs of the case, in recognition of services that he was permitted to offer the nation.

And that, readers, is how the rare and unusual sight of seven reeking turds in jars came to occupy the place of honour in our Baker Street sitting room. Holmes keeps them for their regal ancestry, and as a reminder that even royalty has to shit.

As we left the fine gates of the palace clanking shut behind us, I turned to my colleague.

"That leaves us in a bit of pickle, what?"

"In what way, my dear fellow?" enquired Holmes, his attention understandably concerned by the jars that he was concealing beneath his cape, and anxious not to spill.

"The small matter of a scapegoat. We have to find someone to blame. Vicky said so," I asserted, for I felt, in my British social climbing way, that the preceding exchange had entitled me to talk of her with a certain intimacy.

Holmes sucked at his lower lip for a moment.

"You are right, Watson. Let us hail us a cab and hie forth to Scotland Yard."

We did so, and it dropped us off, conveniently, right next to Lestrade's desk. Holmes had cabled ahead with an abbreviated version of the plot, what little there is. The good inspector would, at first, have none of it.

"But Mr Holmes, he's a completely innocent man! Why would he confess to what he ain't done?"

Holmes chuckled merrily to himself.

"Once Cobblers has been lead down to the cells and kicked in his namesakes as many times as required, I'm sure you will find him most eager to confess entirely to the crime, Inspector, and perchance many others you may find yourself at a loss to satisfactorily explain!"

I beamed on Holmes, as did the Inspector, who was by now dewy-eyed with gratitude.

"Coo blimey! And us here able to help the royals! God bless 'em! They do a marvellous job," said he, and we left him to his pointless rational of our twatty monarch.

Back at Baker Street, Holmes placed the seven jars of royal leavings in their justly prominent position, and sank back into his armchair with a contented sigh.

"A striking, not to say sterling case, I fancy, Watson."

"You fancy Watson?" I said, looking worried. "Oh er, very flattering and all that, old chap, but you know, war wound in the arse and all that. Very sorry but regret, can't oblige."

Holmes chuckled a low, gurgling laugh.

"Very well, my dear fellow. I think I shall retire now for a spot of well-earned slumber. If anyone wants me, I shall be sleeping in the finely attuned pristine neatness of my bedroom."

He left the room and I poured myself a last brandy. The sound of Holmes' door closing snapped my eyes wide open again, and a bellow of "Watson!" headed in my direction. Quickly levering open the sitting room window, I hopped out, forgetting the three-storey drop. Luckily, I landed on Cobblers the Beggar, who was being lead away, and he broke my fall. I felt that he too, in addition to the other shittings, had wrought his nefarious arsery in Holmes' bedroom, too. Or perhaps it was Jack the Ripper. We may never know.

"So, you've got your fingers trapped in the windowsill again, eh?"

"Look! He's found the window!"

"I shall take your word for it, sir, that this is the wrong place, and find the bathroom."

"Sir Frank! You know full well it's my turn with the maid's outfit!"

"Have you ever wondered, Watson, what makes a man turn against his country?"

It was a grave question, and one that treacherous times – and treacherous men – remind us needs an answer. As such I duly pondered while the train rattled past, and the countryside blurred England's glories past the train window.

"Insanity, love of a foreigner, money, revenge, whiffy politics?" I conjectured, knowing full well that there would never be good explanation for some crimes.

Holmes chuckled and looked at me indulgently.

"You are ever the rationalist," he murmured, and then his smile faded. He was silent for a moment as his red-rimmed eyes slid to the window, where they remained fixed for several minutes.

As the train raced along its path, I reflected on the grim tone on which our mission had commenced. Next to us in our carriage were the ashen faces of two significant gentlemen, the Honourable Fortinson Whittam, Secretary to the Defence Minister, and Field Marshal Sir Cyril Kirkland,

It was but a single tense hour since these two gentlemen had beat a worried path to Holmes' door. Although they were clearly of noble stamp, their worried brows told us that this was no time for grovelling and hints about knighthoods.

With but the most perfunctory peck on each of their buttocks, they refastened their trousers and turned to face us. Waving aside all other courtesies and refreshments, they stated their mission.

"Mr Holmes, a matter of gravest national importance has arisen," began the Field Marshal, his fine countenance greyed with the weight of a clearly onerous burden.

The Honourable Fortinson piped up.

"Although we seek representation at the highest level, this must be dealt with discreetly," he intoned with great solemnity, eyeing us both closely.

Holmes inclined his head gravely. I did not move.

"We can say but little at this juncture, for fear of compromise," he continued. Holmes and I both spoke at once, making to protest any possible slur on our patriotic fervour, but the Honourable Fortinson held up a slender hand to silence our blustering words.

"You have no need to explain how trustworthy you are, gentlemen. I am short two five pound notes and a pair of silk boxers since entering the room. However, these are but trifling matters. You must come with me now, gentlemen, and England will thank you for your pains later."

It was thus we came to be on the train to Aldershot, and Holmes asking me what made for treason in the minds of men. It was clear to me he was attempting to gain insight into the situation, for our two esteemed travelling companions had remained tight-lipped throughout.

Holmes and I were sat opposite each other and positioned by the window. Being accustomed to his working methods, I assumed he was ostensibly staring out of the window, but all the while using its mirror image of the inside of our compartment to discreetly assess our clients.

Our two travelling companions spoke in hushed tones, pausing only to turn and pull insulting faces and flick 'v' signs at Holmes, who reddened considerably. One of them went so far as to drape his balls on Holmes' shoulder. It is possible they suspected his subtle observations.

Other than that our journey was uneventful. We alighted at Aldershot with our companions guiding us toward a reception committee. They wore plain grey suits and had dour, determined faces, with hands on their wallets.

The gravest of them spoke first.

"Mr Holmes. Your reputation precedes you. Despite that, we still want your help," he began.

"Unavoidable, really," reflected another with sadness, his face saying that if only there were other ways round these sorts of things, then the world would be a happier place.

"We will perforce say nothing until standing firmly on military soil," the first speaker resumed. "Until then, gentlemen, I must crave your indulgence." He beckoned us into a waiting carriage, which we entered, and remained tight-lipped throughout the journey.

We shortly arrived at the barracks. I, of course, had been around plenty of military bases during the period of my own service, and nothing impresses me more than the sight of Our Boys Being the Best. No sooner had Holmes and I approached the sentry than he shouldered his rifle and waved the butt in our faces.

"Halt, who goes there?" called a determined voice, apparently unaware that he was about to blow his own shoulder off.

"No, no, muzzle to the enemy," corrected the Field Marshal, rolling his eyes. "New here," he explained to us. "Used to be a copper."

"Ah," said Holmes understandingly as we passed the embarrassed sentry. Lagging behind, I tipped him a shilling for his fervour and quietly urged him to tie a sock to the muzzle of his gun so he could tell the ends apart.

There is something about the atmosphere of a military establishment which calls out to the depths in me. This being the 1890's, when British military prestige is the highest in the world, the knowledge that officers are being trained to drink tea calmly while being shelled, to write poetry in the face of grave danger and to ignore the intense cold while generals swill tea and eat warm toast indoors gives me a thrill that radiates all along from my toenails to the tufts of my eyebrows.

Holmes, on the other hand, had never found himself comfortable within the confines of armed forces establishments. A regrettable incident earlier in his career, which I have not chronicled due to his most piteously begging me on the score, shaped this view. I will not go into details, but suffice it to say that four frigates, two destroyers and a command ship made the bottom of the sea their final resting place before Holmes learned it was wiser not to take a bath on naval vessels.

Our reception committee hurried us along to an office, where the Honourable Fortinson and Field Marshal Kirkland stood attending.

"Gentlemen. Thank you for attending at such short notice. You will have gathered, of course, that this is a most unusual and urgent affair. That is, I am afraid, an understatement."

"Perhaps if I could take over," interjected the Field Marshal. "Recently, top brains have designed a secret weapon that would guarantee victory in battle and save many lives.

"Not very sporting," I said sniffily, for I was a stickler for the big, wasteful operations that end thousands of lives unnecessarily. Teaches them character.

"Naturally, top brass were exultant. They considered this would give Great Britain unchallenged military supremacy well into the next century. But, gentlemen, this is where it turns sinister."

The Honourable Fortinson dimmed the lights to add drama.

"The first time this weapon was used, however, calamity struck. It was on the Tabanyama range. The commander of our forces in the region, General Liddell, reported we had every condition from which to expect success, and yet! Calamity struck.

"At this juncture, gentlemen, it may be as well to give you a demonstration of this new weapon before we

74

proceed with our narrative, so that you may fully appreciate the situation."

He beckoned us to follow him outside, which we duly did. A sense of mystery and horror was filling my breast, and one glance at Holmes' face told me that he too was deeply enthralled.

We were positioned at the side of a field, where several official looking observers were waiting with binoculars and clipboards. At the far end of the field was an assortment of painted wooden targets, representing hussars, foreigners, communists and poor people. All in all, a fine selection of targets.

A covered wagon pulled up at one end of the field, from which a sergeant major alighted and two uniformed privates. The privates opened the back and, when the order was given, a succession of six or eight chickens trooped out and stood waiting in a line.

"These pullets are the first of a new breed," whispered the Honourable Fortinson to me. I was unsure of what to say, so I merely smiled and tried to look impressed. One does one's bit for Blighty.

The sergeant major bellowed an order. A unified "bakaw!" was the reply, taken as a signal of readiness. At a flick from his baton, the privates busied themselves with matches and ran from pullet to pullet, stooping to light a fuse as they did so.

I was mystified, and borrowed a pair of field glasses to better observe what was afoot. Focusing the lenses, I was astounded to see that each chicken had been strapped with explosives, which were being primed as I gazed.

A preparatory order was given, then a clear and decisive signal to attack. The chickens advanced, almost in formation, and reached the targets in, what must have been for poultry, record time.

As they neared the targets, the chickens took up what I can only consider a battle cry. The air rang with determined voices that proclaimed "bwark ... bwok

bwok bwok ... bwark ... BANG!" as the first detonated, right on target near a cut-out of a particularly sweaty beggar.

The rest of the chickens exploded more or less simultaneously, annihilating the targets. I caught Holmes' eye, which mirrored the surprise that was doubtless in my own.

"Great Scott!" It was indeed an amazing spectacle to behold, the deadliness of the world's first surface to ground chicken missile.

"Indeed!" replied the Field Marshal grimly. "Simple but deadly. We even baste them with sage and onion first, in case anyone is peckish after the battle."

Holmes and I stood in awe at this fresh example of British ingenuity. Small wonder our little island had enjoyed so large a part in the shaping of world events.

"Gentlemen, perhaps you could rejoin us inside the briefing room?" requested the Honourable Fortinson. Of course we assented.

Once inside, the curtains were drawn shut and cigars were lit, to give a greater atmosphere of intrigue and suspicion, no doubt.

"So, you have seen the might of our new military innovations at first hand," began the Field Marshal. From his grim demeanour I could indeed see clearly that a fresh and terrible development would soon be disclosed.

"Would it surprise you gentlemen so terribly to learn that treason and betrayal in the ranks has left this new weapon useless? Merely a technological breakthrough" – an odd way to describe strapping chickens up with dynamite, but I let it go – "to fall by the wayside due to the untrustworthiness of British soldiers?"

It was an appalling thought. Looking at the Field Marshal, I could see how bitter those vile words must have tasted in his mouth.

Holmes broke the silence that followed.

"Perhaps you should acquaint us more fully with precisely what leads you to this conclusion, Field Marshal."

"Nothing would give me greater cause for hope, Mr Holmes," said he, and at these words I realised things had indeed turned dreadful.

"I believe we mentioned that this new weapon was to be used in our campaigns in Tabanyama, under the auspices of General Liddell. Such was indeed the case. British forces had undertaken campaigns against a resilient and cunning foe, and every resource was considered.

"It was decided to use the chickens, firstly as a means to devastate the enemy lines, and secondly as a means of supplementing the diet of the soldiers, all of whom had been living off paltry rations for some months and in need of a good roast.

"Opportunity to use the new tactic came soon enough, and a strategic point in the enemy lines was targeted. As you may well appreciate, gentlemen, planning was of the essence. The timing of each offensive was vital, as each fuse had to be lit before the chickens charged."

Indeed, I could well envisage the line of gallant men fiddling with the matches while the poultry warheads waited to deliver their deadly and delicious payload.

"It was thought that if this technological breakthrough was as devastating as hoped, then the campaign in that region could be declared a success in a matter of weeks, if not days. However, all was not to be."

At this point a morose silence descended upon the room.

"It is perhaps best if this part of the narrative is continued by an actual eye witness to the facts," observed the Honourable Fortinson, gesturing to a soldier by the door, who disappeared. "This, gentlemen, will be continued by General Simpleton Buller, General

Liddell's second in command, and the leader of the operation in question."

A steadfast, fearless looking man entered the room. He gave the impression of being square-jawed and strong-minded. The door slammed behind him and he jumped perceptibly, while a tiny whinnying fart of fear could be heard. His face betrayed the possibility of having just left something regrettably significant behind him.

Deciding to make the best of it, irrespective of whether we smelt a rat or something worse, the gallant officer rolled his eyes and took the plunge, so to speak.

"We had taken precautions to meet the enemy at a locale that would give us best advantage. All factors appeared to be in our favour. Our foe were preparing to advance when I gave the word to ignite fuses and unleash. The order was followed and the first wave of chickens was off."

General Buller's face contorted for a moment, and some deep inner pain made him wince.

"Then, gentlemen, all unholy hell broke out. Disaster in the ranks. The chickens turned around and charged at their masters, not, as you might imagine, in the fashion of scared pullets, darting hither and thither, wherever they may."

"All the chickens are too well trained for that," observed the Field Marshal to general approval. "Besides, British Army chickens never cut loose."

"Indeed," confirmed Buller. "No, this was a direct and deliberate about face."

Holmes raised a question.

"You mean, the chickens aimed to wipe out their masters and military superiors?"

"Indeed so. It was a precise reversal. My men were besieged by exploding dinners, and the 117th Foot and Mouth were all but decimated."

He shook as a great and terrible emotion threatened for a moment to unman him. I was accustomed to treating battle trauma from my time in India, when many of the soldiers found their mess bills so stressful they ended up living as hermits. As such, I ordered him to shut his eyes and stand on one leg while I blew up a balloon to burst behind his back. Used to work a treat in the old days; at least, I got a laugh out of it.

"I'm not sure that'll help, Watson," soothed Holmes, his keen eye clearly having detected something amiss in the account. He turned to the Field Marshal.

"This is no doubt highly distressing for you all, however I feel we need to approach this rationally, the better to find a solution."

Both the Field Marshal and the Honourable Fortinson indicated their assent. Holmes assumed his most commanding manner and began.

"First of all, how are the chickens directed? What makes them find their targets?" He eyed the assembled military personnel keenly.

"Orders," stated General Buller, to a clamour of agreement.

"I see," said Holmes, his eyes narrowing and an expression of tolerant humour entering his face. General Buller appeared to have cheered slightly at the enthusiastic response to his answer. I began readying my balloon for effective medical bursting when Holmes caught my eye and shook his head.

"And there couldn't have been any mistake in the order?" queried he with the air of one humouring a loon.

"None," came the immediate reply.

"To return to my other point, more specifically," continued Holmes warily, "how precisely do the chickens know who to blow up?"

The senior figures in our tight knit group gathered their heads close together and began muttering intently, one or another occasionally breaking off to glare at Holmes or myself.

"How pray would this serve your enquiries?"

The Honourable Fortinson looked suspiciously at Holmes as he spoke, clearly measuring every smallest nuance of my colleague's deportment in a bid to identify treachery or treason.

"It is essential I know exactly what details may be involved. You have given me the impression that the chickens decided, in one movement, to wipe out the British lines."

"That is true," confirmed the Field Marshal.

"Exactly how it happened," echoed General Buller.

"I see. And are you assuming that somebody else countered the order?"

Some incredulity, and a measure of restraint, could be seen in General Buller's face as he denied this.

"Perhaps the chickens decided to mutiny, then?" mused Holmes, stroking his chin thoughtfully.

At this inflammatory, nay, blasphemous observation, a good deal of outrage was displayed. Dark mutterings of violence or worse could be heard. Above the general clamour of denial General Buller struggled to be heard.

"I can categorically assure you that the British fighting pullet is the best, most loyal and most highly disciplined in the world. My chickens would never consider such a thing."

"Either that or General Liddell, unbeknownst to you, and for his own reasons, gave orders that his own men were to be attacked."

If Holmes' previous remark caused an outcry, this one was greeted with positive outrage. Tables were turned over and papers scattered like confetti in the commotion.

When the general air of chaos and instability had been calmed, and various men of senior rank restrained, the Honourable Fortinson addressed Holmes. His voice was icy, his stare venomous.

"I can assure you, Mr Holmes, that the fate of the 117th Foot and Mouth had nothing to do with treachery, mutiny or confusion."

Knowing Holmes as well as I do, I could tell that his manner was at its most reserved. By this stage, some half a dozen military bruisers had backed Holmes against the wall and were breathing fiercely into his face.

Feeling my place was at Holmes' side, whatever the peril, it was a considerable burden to have to step to one side. From here I could safely observe the aftermath, the better to record an accurate account. I feel my readers deserve it.

Finding himself with perhaps a quarter of an inch of breathing space between life and death by pure indignation, Holmes smiled in a queasy, ingratiating way.

"Perhaps I haven't explained myself at all well, gentlemen. It is my practice, as a scientist of crime, to consider every possible explanation. I follow the facts. I do not make judgements. I weigh details with the dispassionate eye of a surgeon."

"Bollocks," cried someone, and an empty whiskey bottle bounced off Holmes' noggin. I looked to the back of the room, from whence it had been thrown, but could not see the hero in question.

The crowd, however, eased back on Holmes sufficient for him to exhale a moment and lighten the matter. In fact, I swear blind I could hear an easing sound as Holmes' arse relaxed from its red alert posture. Not that military men are prone to expressing themselves with bouts of vigorous cornholing, far from it.

"I have a sworn duty to bring truth to light here, and if that means I ask regrettable questions, well, for the sake of the gallant men of the 117th wantonly served up as legumes, then by Christ, I will ask!"

I noticed a distinct change in the room's mood after this. A murmuring sound passed back and forth, a sound that, while indistinct and as yet inhuman, carried an undertone of respect and understanding that I didn't like to hear.

Holmes, however, was too tense to be aware of this. He was still sweating up like a bastard. His eyes flit from surly bonce to surly bonce, hoping for some kinship to emerge. For myself, watching the proceedings was as enjoyable as farting quietly in a crowded room.

Holmes' eyes found me, and evidently gave him an idea.

"That's Watson! My colleague and chronicler. If anyone can vouch for my methods and patriotism, it is he!"

"Never seen him before in my life," I stated brazenly, disappointed that Holmes might weasel his way out of a good kicking.

It was to no avail. The blood-baying had subsided and the general view appeared to be that Holmes was a necessary evil.

"Thank you, gentlemen," Holmes intoned smoothly, attempting to establish his status once more. "My first thought now is to speak with the commanding officer, General Liddell."

A murmur of assent went round and the Field Marshal nodded his approval. A messenger was dispatched, and Holmes, by way of calming the assembled people, told some diverting lies about his career. I especially enjoying hearing about how he unmasked the jewel thief of Kensington by using a layer of jam, a diamond ring and a wasp's nest. All bollocks, but it passed the time.

The messenger returned looking grave. He whispered in the ear of the Field Marshal, who in turn spoke softly to several people.

"It is likely that General Liddell, if he has anything to hide, will place objections in the way of us talking," said Holmes smugly.

"One might say that, and yet it isn't that simple," observed the Honourable Fortinson, coldly. "General Liddell is dead."

A shocked hush descended on the room.

As a medical man, I was called upon to attend the death. General Liddell was in his quarters and lay arms cast forward, face down on his desk. I made some preliminary checks and gave my report.

"He died from head injuries, many of them. I'd say the weapon was small and round, possibly an egg spoon. From the ten or so thousand impact marks, you could say this was symbolic. Unless the murderer was a breakfast fanatic."

"He's dead!" said Holmes in a small voice.

"Yes, being murdered usually does involve death," the Honourable Fortinson reminded Holmes in a voice weary with patience. "I take it, Dr Watson, that this is murder?"

"Unless he mistook his own head for a boiled egg, yes."

It was a macabre image, this senior military man sat at his desk with some fiend assailant tapping him repeatedly on the head with an egg spoon until he succumbed. A quick look around showed the room was free of bits of toast.

An instant lockdown was put into effect at Aldershot barracks. Holmes and I, as civilians, were required to stay in the Officer's Mess, where we were accompanied by the Field Marshal. The Honourable Fortinson was making arrangements for the coroner and the police, who arrived directly, set up cordons around the base and began interviews.

Sat meditatively and sucking on his pipe, Holmes's face was impassive. The Field Marshal and I looked at him from time to time while playing cribbage for matchsticks. He looking quizzically at Holmes and then raising a subtle eyebrow to me, as though asking what was meant by Holmes' silence.

"He is a rum cove," I whispered reassuringly. The Field Marshal looked at me with one of those "getaway!" expressions.

"Do his methods yield results?" he whispered urgently.

"Always!" I hissed back, although I did not say what type of results.

Any further discussion on the matter was prevented by the arrival of several policemen, accompanied by the Honourable Fortinson. As Aldershot was far from Holmes' regular stomping ground, none of them was familiar. The largest, who was also in charge, spoke.

"As you gentlemen know, a murder has taken place. As this is a barracks, naturally we are sensitive to the fact that several hundred trained killers are on the premises." He coughed and briefly poked into his ear with a distracted pinkie. "Even so, the use of an egg spoon as the murder weapon is somewhat rare."

Holmes rose to his feet and addressed the officer suavely.

"I believe you will find, Officer, that assisting me is the best bet you gentlemen have of successfully concluding your enquiries. I am Sherlock Holmes." He looked to me. I nodded.

"It's true," I admitted. "He is."

"But before," gasped the Field Marshal, "when you said-"

"A cunning ploy to see Holmes get the shit kicked out of him." I shrugged. "I meant well." Which was a lie, frankly.

"Well, Mr Holmes," said the policeman. "I'm sure I'd be very glad of any help. What do you suggest first?"

Holmes was pleased by this acknowledgement of his powers.

"First of all your men must search the barracks for the murder weapon," he began. "Without it a vital clue to the psychology of Liddell's attacker will be lost. Secondly, I must peruse the military records of the deceased and his nearest in rank. The answer, I am sure, lies in the recent past. Or the ancient past. One or the other."

With such expert guidance, the police could only follow.

Holmes warmed to his theme.

"We shall start with General Liddell's background." Fortinson's eyes narrowed. Off this, Holmes added, "In such cases I find that clear insight can be derived from understanding the personal psychology of the individual."

Sending each other expressions of uncertainty, the Field Marshal and the Honourable Fortinson lead the way to the records office. Holmes, clearly delighted to have some real blood and thunder to be getting on with, kept a close pace behind them and tried to keep himself from whistling cheerfully.

"Here are the details concerning General Liddell's career," said Fortinson, after admitting us to a dank, untidy office. He placed a folder before my colleague, who picked through it with delight.

"Crimea, Sudan, India ... quite a distinguished career," murmured Holmes as he flicked over the pages. "I see that General Liddell joined the forces at seventeen, where he served without visible distinction for a time, and then, at twenty five, he suddenly rose from private, second class, to second lieutenant. Why is that?"

The Field Marshal turned a vivid shade of crimson, as though his balls had been grabbed by a cheeky anarchist.

"We, ah, discovered an important detail in his service."

"I see. What was that, pray?"

"Namely that he was heir to the Dukedom of Salford," the old soldier coughed discreetly, trying hard not to look like a berk.

"I see," Holmes murmured. "Of course this was not relevant?"

"Clearly not, of course, good heavens no!" cried all the assembled.

"It was discovered, coincidentally at around the same time, that Liddell was a great soldier," added Fortinson helpfully.

"What had his duties been beforehand?" Holmes asked casually.

"Dusting the bullets and delumping the sugar basin," admitted Fortinson. "But those are vital military tasks!"

"Vital, vital, yes," we all agreed, eyes rolling far and wide.

"And then he made general the following year, having successfully pitched his own tent and made a cut-out tiger from the *Daily Mail*."

"That would be correct, yes. You may think, Mr Holmes," began the Field Marshal, his tone shifting upwards in unpleasantness, "that nepotism was involved. Far from it. His tent was magnificent."

"Of course," Holmes purred, clearing not buying any of it. "Could he have incurred any rancour from the other soldiers, the passed over ones, who could not," here he allowed himself a smile, "use the *Daily Mail* to such purpose?"

The Field Marshal snorted.

"Of course not! This is the British Army, the finest, most disciplined in the world. Mind you, there was one fella who wrote *die posh bastard die* on the barracks wall four hundred times, but we dismissed that as high spirits."

"Then I suggest we start with him."

We were lead to the soldiers' quarters, a dank, urine soaked area of an undiminished bleak pallor. Clearly the regular enlistees were not to be afforded much by way of splendour, and not so much as a wine cork lay around to attest to conduct unbecoming.

The Honourable Fortinson took us down a corridor, escorted by the Sergeant Major, who brandished a bunch of keys with a flourish and opened a door.

"This is the barracks for his unit," we were told.

Holmes entered, carefully examining the array of mattresses and chests. Blowing the dust of one of these, he stooped to examine a small layer of fine grain.

"Watson, if you needed to influence chickens, buy them off, say, and bribe them to forsake their sworn duty, what would you offer?"

I could see he had a point. I once tried to bribe a rooster in Liverpool with ten shillings, without result. If I'd tried grain, who knows?

We exchanged one of these 'important for the plot' glances, and then returned to the barracks, where a number of witnesses Holmes had requested were assembled, waiting.

"I shall be as brief as possible, gentlemen," Holmes began snappily, his voice crisp with authority. "In short, I believe the perpetrator of this abhorrent crime to be within these four walls."

Noises of stirring patriotic blood could be heard, and those listening reattended Holmes, after a mild disturbance, with fervour.

"I shall need full co-operation from you all, for I believe I can readily show the pattern which has lead one of you to commit acts of the most unforgivable and vile nature.

"Field Marshal Kirkland. You have the names of all those who attended military academy with General Liddell. Please share."

"Trotson, Winters, Smalding, Lenister," he read, and then one of the men on the list raced into action, running for freedom.

Holmes' revolver blazed away before he could reach the door, missing the criminal but taking out two fusiliers and a cook from the Gloucesters who was on holiday.

"After him!" cried the Field Marshal, stirring the men's blood to action as Holmes reloaded and apologised to the fallen.

The chase rushed into the corridor and away, I at their heels yelling encouragement as they disappeared into the distance. Holmes, having failed in his attempt to hail a cab to take him from the barracks to the front door, where we could hear the chase resolving, puffed past me waving a magnifying glass.

I am an elderly gentleman, honourably retired from the service due to a bullet in my leg, and I am also a fat bastard. As such I arrived last on the scene, panting slightly and staggering.

The chase had come to an abrupt end. Before me was a writhing mass of soldiers, piled onto what I could only presume was their man, for he was invisible at the bottom of the impromptu scrum.

"You'll talk, hear me, wretched swine?" yelled a sergeant whose face held all the deep redness of intense constipation.

"Richards, how could you?" uttered one of the others pityingly.

Holmes stood aside, for while he is not opposed to violence where necessary – such as when procuring more drinks after last orders – he can supervise as well as the next idle bastard.

"I think you will find this man is merely an accessory, a hired hand brought in for dirty work and betrayal." Holmes addressed the group of soldiers but his eyes were fixed on the disarrayed figure, a man now stooped like a jackal, eyeing Holmes with loathing.

"I did nothing wrong! All I did was seek justice," he hissed.

Before the conservation could add a great deal to the plot, he was hoisted by the armpits and dragged off for interrogation.

"Don't worry, Mr Holmes. He'll tell us everything," said the Field Marshal with dark menace as the woeful figure was lead away.

As the enquiries were due to be of a ruthless nature, we were lead away to partake of a cup of tea and some exquisite cold meat and a very delectable lemon cake.

"The better the army, the worse the food," chuckled the Field Marshal, now a far merrier figure than the tyrant seen previously.

Holmes appeared puzzled.

"Surely these are rather fine provisions for so good an army?"

"That was the view in Julius Caesar's day, certainly. Now, we've found the opposite to be the case. The best soldiers require the finest cooking these days. Take the Queen's Own Hairy Nutters, a crack regiment of homicidal maniacs, none of whom are afraid of sending back a dish if it is not seasoned exactly. Some of the hardest and most feared men have been known to duel to the death over the last slice of partridge terrine."

I nodded my agreement.

"I have heard that to be the case. My old regiment now serves lobster ravioli and entrecote of veal before a big battle or particularly arduous march. But they don't serve claret on Thursdays any more."

"Damn these military cutbacks!" cried the Field Marshal, his fist clenched, eyes bulging in anger.

The mood changed with that remark, and a sour demeanour descended upon the whole room, save for Holmes, who was still attempting convivial persiflage, despite being roundly ignored.

A military porter entered and whispered something. As he whispered to nobody in particular, everyone looked to each other briefly and then ignored this mysterious conduct.

The porter returned a moment later, rolled his eyes, and then beckoned to the Field Marshal who, senior officer that he was, received the news with aplomb. What that august gentleman heard was clearly stirring, for his nostrils flared, his brow thundered and his backside erupted in unholy rage.

He strode from the room, his attendants and the Honourable Fortinson following closely in his wake, and we followed.

"This won't be pretty, Mr Holmes," one of the officers whispered furtively to my colleague. "This one has class aspirations, and we have to break his spirit with them."

"I see," Holmes observed uncertainly.

We stopped at a balcony above a sunken pit, with perhaps half a football field of width. In the centre sat the unfortunate Richards, staring blindly into an intense light. His two tormentors were circling the chair where he sat sunk, a broken man. One of the interrogators clutched a small origami effort, the other grasped a piece of paper as though it were made of turds infected with the plague.

"Look at this, call that a chinchilla?" taunted the first mercilessly.

"A snooty letter?" asked the other, throwing the sheet to the floor, spitting on it and then stamping repeatedly on the offending article.

Their medicine, unusual as it was, had dread effect on Richards, who writhed throughout as though in great pain.

"No no!" he cried, as though in mortal peril. "I am of the elite!"

This came with a piteous sound, like the woes of a three curry man discovering a locked door between him and the crapper.

"He's on the verge of cracking up," the Field Marshal whispered confidently. "I can see it in his elbows," which were indeed quivering much in the way mine do when prescriptions of my special foreskin deodorant run low.

"It wasn't my fault!" he cried out loud, a man possessed. "It was-"

Before he could utter another sound, a pistol shot rang out like a gravestone being dropped down a well full of cymbals. Richards staggered forward, back arched and face staring agonizingly upwards, a man broken by an assassin's bullet.

"Damn it all, we were just getting to the good bit," muttered the Field Marshal in dismay.

We all looked about us, eager to find the man who silenced that accusing tongue, but in the mess of people identification was possible. On the ground nearby lay a smoking revolver, which we went over to inspect.

"As I suspected," Holmes announced, words I usually take to mean 'that surprised the crap out of me.'

"What?" blustered Fortinson.

"Note how this pistol was found by the scene of the crime, and do you know why?"

"Yes, the killer dropped it," answered Fortinson with undeniable logic.

Holmes clicked his tongue and rolled his eyes.

"That is what we are meant to think, but look!"

Ever one for a touch of the dramatics, Holmes tipped the revolver. A lit cigarette fell out of the barrel to general astonishment.

"That is why the pistol was smoking! This is a diversion, no more. I fear we are dealing with a cunning prey here. Field Marshal! Have every man here dusted for fingerprints."

While the thronged assembly was being organised for this, Holmes took me to one side.

"Watson! The killer is Fortinson, and we must trap him."

"What?" I started to bluster, but was interrupted by Fortinson – who had been tying his shoelaces behind Holmes – tearing off.

"Oh shit," muttered Holmes.

"I see," I said, and the restraint of that would make martyred saints look like freewheeling hillbillies on crack.

We chased after him, yelling to the Field Marshal to lend his men for assistance, but they were too busy lecturing Richards' corpse on the importance of loyalty.

Having cleared the main corridor, our man was now racing for the exit. As we turned around the corner, several bullets thundered overhead, narrow misses sent our way by a desperate man.

Holmes and I dived for cover, grabbing our own weapons to return fire. As many new releases in the picture palaces owe much to Oriental action cinema, and we must keep the fans happy, Holmes dived across the corridor gap with a revolver in each hand, blasting away to absolutely no effect whatsoever beyond smashing the crap out of the wood panelling.

A volley of shots was the reply, none finding their mark.

"It seems General Liddell joined the army straight from Porterfield Private School," said Holmes in between shots. "It is my suspicion this Fortinson was there too, and some rivalry developed."

"As good an explanation as any other," I agreed, firing once.

The flurry of gunfire subsided for a moment.

"Tell me straight, Watson," demanded Holmes, no longer the lofty demi-god who once used my tongue as toilet paper and my arse as an ink well. "Tell me, during your time in service, did you ever loot the arsenal?"

"No, why?"

"Because it is my belief that is where Fortinson is heading now!"

That made sense. Holmes' rare good ideas stand out like diamonds in dogshit, but this was one of them. I had to admit it was a corker.

"We must head him off, Holmes. Are the other men free to give chase now?"

Holmes looked over his shoulder at the fine military sight of nearly forty soldiers all covering a revolver, plus cigarette, lying on the floor a hundred yards away.

"It'll have to be us." He looked at me for a minute, his eyes constricting, then placed two fingers in his mouth and whistled at the soldiers, none of whom stirred.

"On my signal!" called Holmes, to complete indifference. Yelling in vain for their attention, using increasingly less salubrious comments, he took a shot at the Field Marshal to get his attention.

"Over here," he cried, wiggling his gun to add gravitas.

The sound of a howitzer being dragged into position by one severely disgruntled, not to mention homicidal, civil servant met our ears.

"Watson! If he gets that set up, we're finished. Run and take him out!"

My answer to Holmes took the form of a long, slow raspberry.

"Arse! Together then, on three."

He counted off and together we charged, me leaving just slowly enough to hide behind Holmes if need be.

The howitzer shells were rather heavier than Fortinson expected, and he struggled to load one as we heaved forward. We got to him and Holmes stuck his revolver up Fortinson's nose accusingly. Realising the futility of his position, he dropped the shell with a clang and eyed us with rare menace.

"The revolver?" queried my colleague.

"Yes, I admit it, Holmes, it was I! I, who had earned my place at Porterfield through good old fashioned brown nosing, watched that slob be given promotion after promotion just because he stands to feature in aristocratic paintings in the near future.

"I always wanted to be a general, but was never well bred enough. Every time I took the general's exam, I found regulations required me to have even closer links to the throne! Damn it all," he cursed.

"When I heard of the chicken offensive, I acted. It required accomplices, of course, men who had also been passed over. And when the truth was almost extracted, I had to act.

"I suppose you, with your extensive knowledge of tobacco, would have realised at once that the cigarette in the gun was of a kind only smoked by those who've attended a minor public school. My only slip," he finished bitterly.

"No," murmured Holmes. There was a slight pause. "I was just going to say it was a nice touch. Ah," he finished off rather lamely, like one who has thoroughly pissed his moment up the wall.

Fortinson thought this over for a moment, mulling his view.

"But wait!" uttered he, bewilderment and rage mixing in his features. "If it wasn't the cigarette, what tipped you off?"

"Well, you did run," Holmes' voice faltered.

A sound hissed loudly. At the other end of the field, looking up from a line of smouldering fuses was none other than the Field Marshal, a smile of malicious glee on his face. From his pocket he pulled one of Fortinson's socks – it was monogrammed – and held its scent before the chickens as they prepared to charge.

(It should be noted they were crossbred from rare hunting pigeons)

Briefly he held up an imperious finger before bellowing out:

"Chickens – attack!"

Holmes and I dashed to safety as the dread onslaught began, unsteadily at first and some pecking for grain en route, but it mattered not. Fortinson, seeing the open beak of justice toddling towards him at an unimpressive speed, stood root to the spot, mouth gaping in horror.

"Bwark bwok bwok bwok bwok."

Covering my head lest bits of traitor should land on my bald patch, I watched the savage blast of the law. The Field Marshal was looking jovial, helping himself to a quick nerve tickler from his gallon sized hip flask.

After a brief explanation to the brass and local police, Holmes and I left Aldershot barracks and its mysterious contents for London, and an altogether different breed of crime.

Some little time later, bolstered by several brandies and the receipt of a reassuringly patriotic cheque, Holmes and I were reflecting on the world from the comforts of our Baker Street flat.

"Heard you how goes life at the Aldershot barracks?" I enquired of my esteemed companion. Holmes inclined his head to think, swirling the remnants in his snifter whilst considering the question.

"I gather the authorities consider the matter satisfactorily closed. They are unlikely to bring charges against the Field Marshal for his hasty dispatch of the traitor, or I should be very much surprised."

I considered for a moment.

"What about the chickens?"

"I gather they were given a full military burial in a casserole, and that their memory was delicious."

"Hurry up with the joint, Watson. I grow impatient!"

"So we see, gentlemen, the laxative is indeed powerful."

The Adventure of the Lingering Stench

It is ever the case, when considering the most esteemed Mr. Sherlock Holmes, that the periods of intense activity, when his quick-fire intellect can light up the sky like a dildo in a convent, are contrasted by a quicksand of the brain that slows his mind like drinking a pint with a floater in it.

For many weeks now the torpors of indolence had rattled his disposition. He spent most days in sloth, staring at the world through the jaundiced, unloving eye of a man who has found his dinner sneezed on.

One such day he broke from his malaise to sit up suddenly. He turned to me with something resembling a gleam in his eye.

"I daresay, Watson, that we must consider you the man of letters of the house. How would you then define the word 'outrage'?"

I paused for a moment and considered this question.

"I would say it meant an event that caused shock or dismay by violating sacrosanct boundaries," I offered.

Holmes smiled, honestly and good-humouredly amused.

"There is much in that view, old friend, of that I am certain. But for one of my profession and tastes, where the commonplace is rare and the ungodly a daily event, such a term offers something of an amusement."

I cast an offended eye toward Holmes.

"Yes, I was thinking only just now how bold and different a figure you cast, sat there eating marmalade and filling in *The Times* crossword with any rude words that fit the space."

He smiled at me indulgently and put aside his pen. Reaching into his coat pocket he produced a telegram.

"Nott-Ffinking, Watson. How's that for a client name?"

I was saved from the ignominy of such an obvious

joke by a knock on the door. Mrs Hudson entered.

"Telegram for you, sir. Just delivered now, it was."

"Ah, I seem to be positively deluged by telegraphic mail just at present. Have a look at my little collection, Watson."

Off his gesture I looked to the mantelpiece and saw a most impressive stack of telegrams.

"Check them all, my dear fellow. A most singular thing, for they all read exactly the same!"

I picked one up and read its contents.

It wasn't me. P.M.

"A most curious and, on the face of it, cryptic note. I presume these are reverse confessions, and if so, to which particular outrage do they relate?"

Holmes waved his hand dismissively.

"Buggered if I know."

"Have you any clue as to this mysterious correspondent, confining himself only to the initials P.M.?"

Holmes shook his head, and Mrs Hudson cleared her throat and offered fresh correspondence.

Holmes ripped open the envelope. He scanned the contents and a faint smile formed over his reserved features. He scribbled off a quick note and handed it over.

"Mrs Hudson, send this note with the boy. Tell him to send a five shilling reply."

"Very good Mr. Holmes," said she pleasantly, opening the under stairs cupboard and taking the boy out of his little box.

"You run off quickly with this, now, Harold," she told him, stapling the note to his face. "Be sure look sharp about you!"

I looked at Holmes, awaiting his explanation of what new client he had, or, considering his secretive nature, what game was already afoot.

"My dear Watson, since we concluded the regrettable business of the Flying Foreskin, I have had little meat for my brain to dine upon. Can you then not understand that I am eager to inspect any interesting problem that may come my way, however trifling? But I think I hear my client now."

A giant creak of straining wood could be heard from outside as he spoke, and we both turned and saw a vast figure from without.

His life history was written in his fine waistcoat and wobbling layer of chins. From his spats to his prominent nose he was a Conservative, a Churchgoer; orthodox, conventional, and a panty sniffer. But some unnerving event had destroyed his manner, leaving its mark in the quickened pulse and darting eye. Even his moustache was askew.

Squeezing the sides of his stomach through our simple door proved difficult, but our man was equal to the task, as was our commendably sturdy doorframe. He navigated his sizeable self into our midst and surveyed us with a popeyed glare.

"Pray sit down, sir," invited Holmes suavely.

He sank into an armchair, which immediately became overstuffed, and waved a top hat full of money at Holmes.

"Pay attention, my man!" he called out. "I have a rum business for you, and a result will not find me ungenerous."

Gracefully detaching Holmes' tongue from the front of his shoe, he began to compose himself. My colleague sat quietly, watching him like a hawk earmarking its lunchtime mouse.

"I have had a most disagreeable experience, Mr. Holmes," he related. "It is a wonder that I am able to speak of these oddities. Even so, I would scarce ask credulity of any but those whose business stretches to the unusual."

"You do not find yourself mislead, sir, for it is indeed far from the commonplace in which I specialise. Pray began your fascinating, lucrative story."

From his arrival, I could not help but admire this gentleman's fine Homburg, which he had placed in his lap upon sitting. He now fiddled with this in a baffled manner, his composure agitated by this unwelcome frustration.

"Recently I have experienced such a rare and unbecoming experience that my heart quickens even now to think on it, and I do not consider myself a man lightly moved."

Eyeing his frame, Holmes and I were quietly agreeing with him as he continued.

"For a man of my station, of my responsibilities, the matter is all the more grave, the more bizarre. I can scarce credit that I am in this position at all!"

The jowls of his face heaved and sank as the emotions of his words bit home.

"Do calm yourself, Mr Nott-Ffinking. You are in the best position you possibly could be."

At that the noise could of about twelve hundred pairs of giant police boots could be heard stomping up our tender stairs.

There was a brief, flustered exchange outside, and then Mrs Hudson appeared in the doorway. Behind her were two police officers, members of the 'man becomes tree' school of thought.

The more senior of the two was a man named Gregson, who at times stood in for vacationing inspectors. Lestrade, I knew, was away on a 'Club 1890' holiday, but whether that referred to the year or the ages of available sexual partners, I was unsure.

"A very good evening to you, Mr Holmes. I am sorry to disturb you, but we have some questions."

"Of course, officer. I am always at Scotland Yard's disposal."

"Thank you, sir. We have come, however, to speak to your visitor, Mr Nott-Ffinking."

"I assume you traced him through the telegram?"

The more talkative of the two coppers bowed his

head. Holmes turned once more to our guest.

"Please listen to me carefully, Mr Nott-Ffinking, for I have your best interests at heart," said he, never taking his eyes off the hat full of cash. "I suggest you ignore the fuzz and continue with your story exactly as it would have been. Watson, I believe a quick gargle would do our guest no harm at all."

I filled a glass and passed it to him. He took it from me, glancing the policemen with some trepidation, and drained it at a sip, such were his nerves.

"I had been visiting some friends of mine in Surrey, near Reigate. I am a bachelor, and being of a sociable disposition have cultivated a wide circle of friends, whom I visit regularly.

"I was waiting at the railway station, awaiting my return to the metropolis. A young gentlemen approached me and asked if I had been staying at the Thomason household, which I had. They were great friends of his, so he said. I saw no need to doubt his word.

"He told me much of himself. He had of late been adventurous on the seas, traversing near a quarter of our broad globe. His skin was tan brown and he told me tales of broad brimmed straw hats. He spoke almost perfect English, despite being a Cockney, and he was a most peculiarly attractive young man."

Our guest shifted somewhat uncomfortably in his chair and discreetly rearranged his hat.

"On the arrival of the train, he bade me fond farewell. I rose to collect my belongings and alight to the train when, and oh! but here I burn in shame," his face indeed had reddened to the extent that passing coachmen could be heard crashing in the street, such was the glare. "My trousers fell down. Quite inexplicably, for I always secure them with a stout and capable belt tightened as far as my fulsome waistline will allow.

"Picture the scene, gentlemen. A full and crowded railway platform, with a great variety of people attending to their lawful business, and me with the pale and hairies on display, with only the taunting sight of my coiled trouserage gathered by my ankles, my self respect scarce three feet away, but such a distance, and so great a gulf, that I feel I may never again fully recover the dignity which was rent from me so hideously!"

At these words of such a dread occurrence, he, being already robbed of his dignity, reached forward and rested his head in his hands. A series of dry convulsions wracked his system.

Dispensing with the glass, I picked up the brandy decanter, put a straw in it and handed it to him.

Holmes looked grave, and stroked his chin thoughtfully.

"It is a more serious matter than even that, sir," intoned one of the policemen, his tone grave. "I fear it's murder! You see, one of the witnesses, an elderly lady of scholarly disposition, saw the outrage and reported it to Scotland Yard. She was taken into hospital immediately following the disgrace and has since succumbed to the shock."

"This is terrible! I swear, upon all that I hold dear, that I was no party to the dread event. I considered the propriety of the covered leg, and fully concealed shorts, to be the very essence of Englishness. Such a disaster is beyond my comprehension, sirs, utterly!"

"No," said Holmes evenly. "There I will disagree with you, Mr Nott-Ffinking. I think I see where the truth may be ascertained. Reigate is, as you know, home to one of the largest belt manufacturers in the world, Bullborough's. I think Watson and I do good work by catching a train to those parts and instituting enquiries."

Our guest looked at Holmes with an expression of pure gratitude.

"Oh, I pray you, Mr Holmes, do all that you can, to uncover the truth behind this wretched tragedy. I place my full support behind your endeavours."

As the policemen the unfortunate Mr Nott-Ffinking to his feet and handcuffs, Holmes sprang up from his chair.

"Be of good cheer, sir, for you have one of the few specialists in such matters on your side. Shall we call it one top hat full of money per day? Very well then."

Later that evening, Holmes and I were discussing the unfortunate Mr Nott-Ffinking.

"It is an unfortunate matter that this man, who I consider entirely innocent owing to his swollen money bags, is currently suffering incarceration."

I thought on this as I imbibed another brandy.

"Surely you have no real question on the matter, Holmes? He has admitted being out on a railway platform with insecure trouserage, and now an elderly member of the public is dead."

Holmes inclined his head with a tolerant half smile.

"What you say is true. However, I feel any stretch of imprisonment is too great for our man. I have no doubt he is totally innocent," Holmes' voice grew somnolent as his head leaned further back into his armchair, "and doubtless I shall prove so with," he stifled a yawn, "tireless investigation."

"Spare no energies," I said approvingly, hoisting another cushion behind my back and relighting my cigar.

Sleep had almost claimed me for her own when the bell rang. Thinking with horror that it was last orders, I had half arisen from my chair before I realised where I was.

Sinking back down again, my patience got the better of my curiosity and soon I was being woken from the first shallow layer of sleep by Lestrade. He was dislodging rain aplenty from his police issue raincoat and was shaking his head.

"Bloomin' heck, Mr Holmes," he said in a gormless way. "If it ain't the last flood out there, I've gone dropped a clanger."

Holmes acknowledged the inspector with a dismissive wave of his hand. Without opening his eyes, for such, I should imagine, was the demand of his great concentration, he pointed a long finger down at the evidence drawer.

With a deferential, "Oh, I see, then," Lestrade bestowed his paperwork. He doffed his rain hat – which landed about fourteen pints of water right into the vulnerable bit of my slippers – and left.

The following day Holmes rose at dawn, sent an encouraging word to his client at Her Majesty's Pleasure, and went promptly back to bed.

We breakfasted late that day, and I was still cracking open boiled eggs when Holmes began emptying his evidence drawer. He appeared to be looking for something, and indeed held up many a piece of paper in hope, only to be disappointed. I would say he continued with this for at least three eggs.

"It is here somewhere, I will swear upon it!" he kept insisting, although I had long since given up on listening to him and was making my Christmas card list.

"Watson, seen you a telegram?" I rolled my eyes, for when Holmes starts tinkering with verbiage, it is time to worry.

"I saw it this morning, when I sent an encouraging missive to Mr Nott-Ffinking. It is vital!" With that he began dislodging sofa cushions, and pointing his magnifying glass at everything in sight. The cat became rather annoyed and, quite properly, piddled in Holmes' deerstalker.

It became a dread utterance in our homestead to mention the word 'telegram.' I had considered posting guards at either end of Baker Street, or at least outside 221b, to prevent further strain from ailing my colleague.

Holmes, when mid chase, had a habit of spoiling my robust laziness. I had not shot my leg in the Far East without good reason, and his persistent, straining energy was irksome.

I decided to employ the methods I usually do on such occasions. Delivering a swift boot to Holmes' stooping rear, then looking angelically innocent as he turned wrathfully around, I left the flat. Heading for Soho and a fun afternoon with the baby oil and my army pension, I resolved to return later and swipe the narrative from what I could piece together from his notes.

Upon my soggy return some regretful hours later, a deep sense of malaise turning me hollow, I found no little police activity in my path.

Lestrade was busy testing the world's first mobile telephone. I had heard him discuss this several times of late, and in such a way as to make the listener weary. It did indeed appear the most wondrous device, allowing as it did the user to receive or make calls whilst mid perambulation on the streets of London.

"It'll work in the country, too, he boasts," Holmes commented on the matter, "once they can find a lead long enough. As it is he keeps getting wrapped around lampposts. They call it 'the canine's companion' at the Yard, or so I am informed."

Such ideas had been discussed the fortnight before Lestrade's holiday, and it occurred to me that even the smallest of distractions was preferable to the sorry state before me now.

I found Holmes with his face on a pile of missives, eyeballing them closely. They had been spread across the tabletop so that a pertinent section of each was visible. Crouching low by the table I looked up at the strange scene of this, most uncelebrated of detectives, fixing his full mental powers on the clues before him.

Clearly these were the fruits of his search, namely all manner of completely irrelevant bits of paperwork spread before his hawk gaze.

A twist of paper sticking out of the marmalade drew my attention. I unravelled it, sucking the excess marmalade off my thumb.

"Unless five thousand pounds is placed in used bags at the crossroads in Piccadilly Circus, the Prime Minister's trousers will fall down in Munich."

What a big pile of wank, I thought to myself, rolling the eyes. Without wasting another second on the daft note, I crumpled it into a neat paper ball and tossed it onto the table.

Immediately Holmes' antennae quivered. He fell upon the note, straightened it, and devoured its contents.

"This is it, Watson!" said he, a feverish tone entering his voice as he chewed. "We must move swiftly, for there is no time – no more time – to be lost," said he in a rare moment of self-correction.

"Rush you out into the street and call a hansom, for we must make haste," said he, oblivious to my previous absence. Such is the role of the sidekick, I said to myself with a sigh. I left just in time to see Holmes pick up his hat and drench himself in cat piss.

The day at least has that going for it, I thought, with a wink to the cat.

Our hansom pulled up at Downing Street to face a grim, near martial scene. A thick covering of policemen lined each side of the street, and clearly a major crisis had arisen. My first thought was of assassination by some nefarious power, but then I remembered the odd words of the telegram.

Could it be that such an abundance of police manpower was due to a threat, however ridiculous, against the stability of the Prime Minister's trousers?

Lestrade, easily noticeable thanks to his incredibly long telephone lead, walked over to where we stood. Holmes immediately assumed his habitual manner of superiority, and I crouched down to avoid flying bricks.

"There's not a moment to be lost, Mr Holmes."

"Then for show me inside without delay," snapped Holmes, imperiousness itself now that the appropriate

106

paperwork had been found.

We found ourselves ushered through the police cordon surrounding that famous front door. I had never before been privileged to gaze so close on the halls of power. My discreet admiration was sufficient to prevent me from trousering the odd painting; that and the beady eyes emanating from a severe rank of coppers.

Holmes and I were shown into a distinguished waiting room; a magnificent chamber with majestically high ceilings, gilded furniture and red carpet on the walls. Had the Soho palace I visited earlier shown such poor taste, I'd have left without the merest golden shower.

We were left alone for but a few moments when the imposing black doors swung upon and in walked the unmistakeable figure of Holmes' impressively bulked brother Mycroft. This gentleman was a legend among gannets, and is rumoured to have single-handedly finished off the entire buffet at the Sheridan Club in one sitting, table and all.

"Holmes!"

"Mycroft!"

Ah, the wonders of the British public school system, I said to myself. I had been warned that Mycroft would only refer to his brother by surname, such was his devotion to the stiff upper lip. This is the type of stunted formality has made us the envy of the civilised world.

Mycroft's tall, dignified presence was topped off by a head of such polished radiance that for several minutes I could only look at him through my fingers.

He spoke with a booming voice.

"Gentlemen, allow me to present to you the greatest naval expert in the world, Sir–General Maving–Maving."

A fine figure of the British old guard walked in. He was tall and his posture ramrod straight. He was clad in the manner of civilian suiting that so easily marks an ex-military man out of his professional attire.

What marked him more for particular personal

greatness, however, was his most glorious moustache. This finest of specimens was a wide mass of bristles, the like of which could cripple a man if it landed on his foot.

Awed, Holmes and I could only look upon the fine article with wonder. It seemed to ennoble all who stood in its presence with a rare beatific light.

"Good evening gentlemen. I daresay my colleague has explained my speciality to you; however I fear I haven't the time to examine your navels today and ensure they are all present and correct."

"I assure you they are. Is that all we are here for?"

"No. I speak of a much graver affair," said he with ashen face.

"We've already had the plot, thank you, Sir-General," said Holmes affably, looking at his pocket watch with a chuckle of satisfaction and noting that we were indeed making rare progress.

His noble eyes turned mellow from above the vast, backbreaking hair of his upper lip.

"Then god speed your efforts, gentlemen!"

Early the next morning Holmes and I could be found making our way to the station and catching the earliest train to Reigate. Throughout the journey Holmes was silent, immersing himself in a volume on wasp keeping. From his intent, studied demeanour I knew there was little to be gained in conversation.

I passed the time enjoying the scenery, wondering if my friend was ever going to get a life.

We had spent several days' toil investigating the matter, and once more I observed the rigours of the detective process when practiced in its true form.

Holmes had worked ceaselessly, as was his wont when close upon the scent of a dread crime. He worked all the hours god sent, or at least two of them.

Studying the belts of all manner of London personages had become with him an obsession. Soon he became the country's leading authority on such matters as tension, pullage and, most vital of all, security.

As we alighted from our train at Reigate station, it was with the air of one who anticipates great things that I packed up Holmes' portable narcotics kit and small rubber chicken.

Hailing a cab, we made straight for the beltmakers, Bullborough's. Noting a number of suspicious persons dotting the road, many of them posting letters, walking dogs or simply looking at us with mild curiosity, we proceeded with some caution upon arriving at our destination.

A brisk and fierce wind whipped up around our faces, causing us both to wince. My cheeks were rapidly becoming chapped, so I hoicked up my trousers.

"Just researching the crime, old chap," I said to Holmes by way of explanation. His face pulled long and thoughtful, eyes to the side, and he began hammering fearlessly at the door in his unsubtle way.

The housekeeper answered the door and showed us inside.

"I'll let the master know you are here, sirs," she said pleasantly. "Is there anything I might bring you?"

"Oh, the culprit, the plot and some clues would be nice, thank you kindly."

Holmes spoke dryly and I suppressed a chuckle at his dry wit. The housekeeper, however, did not react.

"I shall bring them directly, sirs. Would you like your clues with milk or cream?"

At no response from either of us she left to fetch the master of the house, muttering something about a pair of bell ends as she went.

The door flew open and a surly browed man with a great face full of hair met us. His eyes popped forth with a prominent red in the whites and a glare in the browns. His moustache blanched up and down and his great beard wobbled with vexation as he glowered.

"Good day to you, sir. I am Sherlock Holmes."

"And I am buggered if I care!" roared he, his facial hair puffing out and retreating like an anenomi swimming away.

"We are here to investigate a matter of national importance," offered Holmes with unmoved hauteur.

The man's face grew redder, a feat I should have scarce thought possible, and he sucked in a good mouthful of whisker.

"You've arrived right in the middle of buckle straightening season, you great nit. Any interference with my business at this stage, and the trousers of the great and the good will dig into their middles. Can you live with that, sirs, can you?"

Impressive though this unexpectedly delicate concern was, it did nothing to daunt my colleague or squash his demeanour. He stood his ground in the face of Bullborough's coarse tirade.

"I must direct you to admit us to your premises, for the warrant I have in my pocket guarantees the arrest of all I finger."

The man's brow wrinkled into an even darker mask of hatred as he misunderstood Holmes' poorly chosen words. His person grew with the preparations for violence, shoulders rising and muscles bristling with anticipation.

"Very well, sirs," said he after inspecting the paperwork Mycroft had given us. With great effort to restrain his mounting anger, he stood before us trembling with rage.

"I shall say this, sirs. Your presence had better be a subtle one, for I have much vital work that needs be done to secure the trouserage of the gentry."

He eyeballed my companion closely, but Holmes would not be moved.

"I fear I will stop at nothing. Until our investigation is at a close, you will have to co-operate with every particular."

"I will go where I please and I will also say my piece! This is my business here, my livelihood, and what affair it is of you ugly bastards, I've no idea. I will not suffer any big ponce with a silly hat and two foot of pipe jeopardising my business, so you see here now!"

It was an impressive speech, delivered with plenty of fire and gusto, and left an impressive amount of froth lingering in his beard.

Holmes eyed him impassively and rose smoothly to the occasion.

"You will find me no intrusion, sir, without the direst of causes, for my affair heralds the nation's goal, and no one man shall stand in my way!"

"Is that so?" cried he with a sneer. Reaching down he plucked the poker from its resting place by the coalscuttle.

Brandishing it menacingly before Holmes' bulging eyes, he braced it in his two great fists and bent it over into a curve.

He tossed it into the fireplace with a leering smile in our direction. Holmes waggled his eyebrows and took the challenge. Picking it out of the grate, with a sudden effort Holmes managed not to straighten it.

Embarrassed by his feeble ineptitude, I watched as he struggled with the bent poker, growing redder in the face as he hefted and strained.

Bullborough watched with a jubilant smile, a sinister flicker of delight illuminating his dark face.

Piggy eyes bulging with glee, he tweaked Holmes' nose and pulled his hat down so hard on his head it looked like a deerstalker necklace. I inadvertently managed to be looking away as he stuck two fingers up at me, whereupon he left the room with a threat and a great thunderous slam of the door that spun the ornaments.

We were silent for a moment, then Holmes looked at me from within the realms of his tattered deerstalker. Crooking a thumb at the door, he sidled out and I followed, also sidling.

Outside, Holmes gradually began to resume his old manner.

"It is my belief that this gentleman is a suspicious character, and one to observe rather more closely," said he, after the fashion of one imparting great wisdom.

"You mean, the huge beetle-browed giant of a man? The one who twists bits of metal as though they were made of putty? The fellow who expressly stated he would ruin both our marriage prospects if he ever sees our twatty forms again?"

Holmes thought for a moment and then nodded his head.

"Yes, that's the one. The man who, I hope you noticed, I deliberately mislead into believing I was weak and incapable of performing the same feats as himself, for such is my great game."

"Of course," said I, brushing bits of shredded hat from his coat. "That's totally convincing."

Some hours later, after several large brandies and my distinguished colleague had very much rewritten the occurrence in his head, we made our way back to the beltmaker's.

" ... and I gave him a left, and a right, and then I got him by the neck and ..." said he to a passing lamppost.

I gave Holmes a reassuring pat on the back as he finished his victory dance, ending knees on the deck, arms waving overhead.

After a brief calming period and a quick application of Dr MacNamee's patented deep breathing easy rest shoulder rolls, he resumed a version of his professional manner, slightly pissed.

Instead of grappling once more with the formidable Bullborough, a more subtle line of enquiry was pursued.

We chose our moment to snoop carefully, knowing that the stentorian beltmaker would be out that evening, making merry at The Throaty Belch. This sterling piece of information had been observed by Holmes, upon offering his housekeeper a fiver to spill the beans on his movements. It ranked the equal of any feat of detective work I had seen him pull, and I raised my glass high to his good sense.

Necessarily, our route took us past the very same ale emporium. It was a hushed moment without a certain shame to know that we not acting out of wet trousered cowardice, but only taking prudent measures to conceal our heroic actions.

We crept round the front of the by now boisterous public house. Holmes, a fresh deerstalker in position and keeping his great brain warm, sneaked along ahead of me.

Stepping with some trepidation, we made our way along. Thrillingly we had edged almost the first half of the pub's length when a well-refreshed figure appeared in the doorway. He, clearly of an amenable frame of mind while mid imbibation, looked upon us with a smile that was affability itself.

For a moment we relaxed, smiling courteously with Holmes pointing at my arse and making 'fold it' currency gestures between his fingers.

It was a mistake. A look of 'aha!' crossed his face, and for us the realisation that discovery was imminent. The merest cry of attention from him could find us at the mercy of a pissed up Bullborough, Holmes and I immediately took up our defensive positions.

Holmes pulled a duck from his pocket, secreted there in the case of any such eventualities, he later informed me, without conviction, and began kissing it on the beak and crooning over its fine brown feathers.

"Oo, me duckie-oo, speckled arse," said he with a hefty twang.

Our observer blinked several times and called out to us incoherently. We mumbled gibberish back and I, impersonating something of the outdoor eccentric, immediately began chewing straw and rolling my eyes.

It is possible that my tailored waistcoat and bowler hat may have undermined my disguise, but one learns to make do in the field. An extra cheesy smile on my face, and I was ready to go.

I had been rocking back and forth on my by now considerably inflamed ankles, and was ready to straighten my position when Holmes took my elbow in a grip of iron. The moment could have blown our cover, but Holmes artfully placed a cunning veil of misapprehension about his features.

With a final piece of incoherent gibberish, Holmes succeeded in driving away our observer, who staggered back to the bar with a grunt of approval.

Finding no further objection to our progress, we slipped past the pub and made our way into Bullborough's back yard. Checking there were no witnesses, Holmes produced a jemmy from his pocket and carefully smashed all the windows in.

"That'll teach him to threaten me," he said with a chuckle. I rolled my eyes, which was wasted in the dark, I suppose.

Levering the back door open with a spoon, Holmes and I crept in. We made our way through the first two rooms.

"Hist, Watson, for I know where I am going," said he with a confident wink, tripping over the cat and inadvertently butting the dinner gong. Once the colossal din had subsided, and the ornaments had stopped rattling, I stubbed my toe on Holmes' arse and we proceeded to the main point of our search.

We walked into a fine drawing room with an elaborate green baize motif. It was rather like breaking into a snooker table. Knowing as we did that right was on our side, we quickly pocketed a number of fine objets d'art to recompense us for any trifling inconvenience.

I gathered my nerves and refastened my trousers.

"No time to worry about that, Watson," whispered Holmes. "If you have any apprehension about the safety of your ring piece, may I assure you that in this part of the country the major houses have particularly magnificent toilets."

I followed Holmes taking small comfort, and even

that offset by the strange knowledge my colleague possessed. I looked around me at the great room, wondering what clue or artefact would point Holmes in the right direction.

The door closed quickly upon us, and a chilling icy voice, like footsteps dancing on my grave, warned us of our peril.

"Stay perfectly still, gentlemen. I am a crack shot, and as the pair of you are breaking into my house I am confident I can use my weapon with the full support of the law."

Rapidly sobering, Holmes and I both followed the gesture of the gun barrel, to our astonishment, saw the wrinkled, evil walnut face of Professor Moriarty.

The shivers that silky, cold voice had prickled had been no mistake. My senses had been warning me, and now I saw how right they were.

"I assure you, gentlemen, that the end of tonight, and your lives, will soon be upon us."

Holmes faced him with steel in his eyes and a quaver in his voice.

"If any attempt is made upon my safety, you will surely answer for it!."

I looked at Holmes with lingering distaste.

"And that of Watson too, of course," he said, an ingratiating fawn in his voice while edging behind my voluminous person. "My agents know I am here."

Moriarty's features wrinkled into a cold sneer.

"No they don't, Mr Holmes, for my agent saw you outside the pub attempting to have your way with a duck. Your private life is immaterial, however. Your enquiries into the truth behind the falling trousers have lead you here, to the heart of my operations, to the unmasking of my destructive scheme."

"I fear you are too sanguine, my dear professor. Confident as you are that I was right upon your trail, it is here that you make your error, for I had actually no idea!"

Holmes' moment of triumph may have seemed a little baseless, as the fiend Professor looked momentarily nonplussed and then waggled a finger at Holmes in triumph.

"An interesting admission, my dear Holmes."

Holmes' response was one of studied contempt.

"I wonder why you insist on calling me 'my dear Holmes' during the whole routine? It's obvious you don't like me."

These words were callow but calculated. Though they may have sounded petty, they took the professor by surprise.

"A good point. Perhaps I shall call you vile Holmes? Nitwit Holmes? Bighead Holmes? Mr I-never-got-a-doctorate-much-less-a-professorship Holmes?"

Holmes became at once a model of aloof restraint.

"I fear, professor, you may have overlooked the not inconsiderable role you played in the matter."

"This is true. I scribbled all over his equations and drew a pair of tits on a fraction," he said to me by way of explanation.

"The exam board refused to accept my papers," Holmes confirmed moodily.

"Although they did say it was by far the best work you had ever presented," said the professor with some mild satisfaction. "But now to the matter at hand."

Here the devil rose once more in this most fiendish of fiends.

"I shall not impose too greatly, gentlemen. If you would find it convenient to take a chair, my assistants will bind you."

Following the point of his revolver, it was impossible to resist. We sat under the auspices of the professor's gun and were tied hand and foot by surly, moustachio'd henchmen.

It was all very predictable.

Holmes was confidence and savoir-faire personified, once he'd had a little cry.

"Do you suppose, my dear professor, that I have been unaware of your increasingly elaborate attempts to assassinate me?"

Holmes faced his nemesis with a quizzical, sardonic eye. The other one was quivering like the Dickens and asking for its mother.

"That apple pie was meant for someone else," he said darkly, peering around the room through eyes narrowed into slits.

"What apple pie? I referred to the random and increasingly erratic gunshots which have been dogging my footsteps all over London these last few weeks."

Moriarty's face fogged with confusion.

"Nothing to do with me, Holmes. Must be some of your distinguished and no doubt entirely satisfied clients."

He cleared his throat and gave a theatrical wave of his hand.

"I arranged for a small distraction that would deliver you to me. It was absurdly easy, knowing as I do how fascinated you are by trousers falling down."

I could feel Holmes stiffening next to me, but decided not to make the obvious joke.

Moriarty continued.

"Imagine my delight in knowing that I could deceive and diminish Mr Sherlock Holmes himself, and all merely by sending him a telegram saying I had not done it! Ha!"

He finished on a high note of dramatic villainy, and his words struck such a blow that Holmes had achieved what can only be described as a full twelve on the 'Eyebrows of Destruction' scale. I keep this useful chart on the wall of my study, marking the appropriate squares with a coloured pencil the height of that days' eyebrow haulage.

"So it was you who sent all those telegrams!" said Holmes, his eyes wide with shock like a little boy who has been offered stolen jam.

An expression of pure mystification crossed Moriarty's face, showing that Holmes had done something to turn the tables. I for one cheered it.

"Who did you think it was?" said he, genuinely mystified.

However, the edge afforded us by Holmes' outstanding dickheadery was short-lived, for the diabolical professor's mood of devilish evil swiftly returned.

"No matter. I had little hope that you would get far, matching your pitiful peanut brain against the might of my radiant marbles."

It was true that the overhead lighting reflected fiercely off the bilious cue ball of Moriarty's noggin. With the fierce glint of the triumphant master criminal twisting his face to glowering manic hatred, the softly burning candles less than a foot overhead cast an eerie glow over the room. It was a bonce disco for the especially strange.

"It is not a matter of glare," replied Holmes cheekily. I was again mightily pleased with this indefatigable bulldog stand.

It impressed Moriarty but little, I fear.

"I suspect you are so far from the truth you believe the crime you are trying to prevent regards to falling trousers. Permit me a little red herring, for as we speak, my operatives are removing England's finest fighting moustache from the sleeping figure of one Sir-General Maving-Maving."

I should imagine Holmes has not been so surprised since he caught his elder brother watching vile naughtiness on the magic lantern. Mycroft told me about it, and I must admit it afforded me the slightest of hearty gut laughs.

The plot against the moustache, though, was a new and terrible development.

"I shall not weary you with details, however. Suffice it to say that you have delivered yourself here to me, and now you must pay!"

He swept from the room with his customary diabolical laugh. From our bound position, we could only look on in horror as an assistant unveiled the mechanism for our death with a hideous chuckle.

Before us sat a huge pile of dynamite, complete with hissing fuse, and a rapidly disappearing one at that.

"Bugger!" we said in unison.

There was a meaningful pause, followed by a telling squirt.

"Sorry, old stick," I said, face crumpling in remorse. "I'm afraid I've let go of a brown package."

It took a brief moment for the complete, terrible horror of these dread words to strike home.

"Oh nice," said he, and I could tell from those few syllables that his crest had truly fallen. "Oh terrific! Of all the bumbling sidekicks in the world, I get the one who makes fudge the moment danger arrives."

I could only agree.

"A full Prescott, I am afraid." It was as well to appraise him of the full horror of the situation before it reached up his nostrils and crossed his eyes.

A most unpleasant sensation of leakage was upon me from behind a moment later. I was sore astounded that my vastly capacious trousers could not contain the outpourings my bottom had let slip.

To my intense amazement, the ropes slipped from my wrists.

"Holmes, I have come undone!" I cried joyfully.

"That's an understatement," said he witheringly.

"Oh, well, if that's how you feel, then I'll be off," I said.

I stood from my bonds and looked pityingly at the still fizzing fuse. With a cheery smile to Holmes I made for the door, turning back to luxuriate momentarily in the sight of Holmes sat frantically trying to blow out the fuse.

Of course I would not leave my celebrated friend in such a position, for the loss to humanity in general would have been too great. However, I did have time to sit down for a relaxing pipe and a quick bash at the crossword before untying him.

"Pleasant weather, eh, Holmes?" said I with a chuckle. He was still huffed in the face from the severe effort of trying to blow out his fate.

"Good to have a bit of exercise, what?" I chortled at him, noting with approval the rich light of disparagement that flickered in his bulging eyes.

Noting how the wick was nearing its destination, I plucked him by the sleeve and helped him to his feet.

"Through here, I believe, old fellow," he announced, taking control once more. He went to the bookcase and plucked at the spine of a volume. Immediately a doorway opened.

"How did you know about that?" I queried, mystified.

"I watched Moriarty," he shrugged, for once not puffing himself up. "You were too busy shitting yourself."

We made our way through the door and away from danger. Stood in a murky corridor, its air stagnant but mercifully fresher than that we left, both of us let out a breath of relief.

"Well, Watson, we are free!"

With that heartfelt exclamation, a warm flood of relief showed through Holmes' icy features, much reminiscent of the expression he held at the happy conclusion of the Frustrating Affair of the Missing Toilet Paper.

We had taken barely two steps when a familiar voice echoed down the passage.

"Yes. At any moment the bomb will detonate and Mr Holmes will be no more. Luckily my library is bomb proof. I shall hear a most satisfying noise shortly, and then nothing will stand in my way!"

"It's the professor!" I hissed quietly. Holmes nodded impatiently and checked his pockets for firearms.

Moriarty was still speaking into the telephone when

Holmes made his entrance.

"You clever fiend," said he, brandishing his revolver with venom.

("Well brandished, old chap! I said to him with approval. He winked back and pulled a quick 'yeeks!' face, then resumed eyeballing the prof with his best gimlet stare.)

For a moment Moriarty appeared confounded, then his old damnable self took over.

"Very clever, Mr Holmes. It would appear I underestimated you."

His voice tailed off as he noticed the brown stains on my hands.

"A bag of chocolate melted in my pocket," I informed him haughtily, wafting away some flies.

"Quite so," said he, and then burst from his chair in a rictus of flailing movement. He flung a bust of Napoleon at Holmes, which bounced harmlessly off his head. The revolver fell to the ground. In a trice the professor had opened another secret compartment and was in the act of disappearing over the threshold.

A stone was kicked back by his shoe, and it plummeted over the edge of what sounded like a vast drop. Moriarty looked back for a second. It was to be his undoing.

For one lingering moment he struggled to correct his balance, flailing helplessly against his fate as the power of good overcame his vile infamy. He fell.

"Aeiiiii!" called a shrieking voice, followed by a deep plopping splash.

Holmes stood there, trying to look like Humphrey Bogart.

"Ah ha, only kidding," called the professor through cupped hands, appearing briefly in the dim light at the end of the passageway. He then made an impressive raspberry noise, thumbs to his ears and fingers wiggling, before scuttling on his evil way.

Holmes ground several teeth and gestured at me to

follow him. Angrily he strode from the house, giving the deceptively refined surroundings a deft toot from his arse.

"We must move quickly, Watson," said he briskly. "In a matter of hours the Professor will be on the seas, and then England's finest fighting moustache will be on the continent, destined for foreign lips."

"Egad," I muttered in low horror.

"Indeed. Should any representative of half a dozen countries be seen sporting the General's moustache, then British military prestige will be tarnished and our borders will be subject to pillage and invasion.

"I know of half a dozen guileful foreign agents, each capable of handling so delicate a delivery. It is to their doors we must repair now. If we fail, then England is destined for many years of pointless, unnecessary, but completely splendid wars."

His words did no exaggeration. Diplomacy is not to my fore, but it was easy to see the ruinous impact of such fine British foliage being used against us. My mind flit back to the ruinous foundation of the Boer War, when the simple but exploited happenstance of a misplaced monocle spelled doom for a generation.

It was true – the facial hair leak must be plugged, and with all speed. Trundling along at my fastest rotation, to keep pace with Holmes' gallant stride, I hastened to play whatever small role I could in this most earnest of patriotic errands.

We caught the next train back to London, wiring ahead to Mycroft and appraising him of events. Several tense hours later we alighted at Victoria, and stood for an eternity waiting for a cab. Then, inspired by an event we had both seen in a recent theatrical production, we leapt aloft a pair of passing beggars and waved pound notes before their bulging eyes as we hot footed it to Pall Mall.

Inside the hallowed portals of his club, Mycroft surveyed Holmes with angry, disappointed eyes.

"Fool! Incompetent boob!" said he, looking at his brother as though the other were caught sniffing saddles in the women's Penny Farthing sheds.

"There has been another public debagging, and this time against one of the very highest personages!"

Against our bewildered expression, he raised his significant bulk from the armchair with a mighty leap, so great was his vexation, and strode to an occasional table.

Grabbing from this a newspaper, he held it aloft like St George confronting the dragon with a shining sword.

"Behold for yourselves!" he urged, a note of hysteria in his voice.

We looked, and both took a synchronised step back in horror.

> "Prime Minister drops trousers at Women's Institute. Mass outbreaks of fainting, hysteria, lust."

"So!" gaped Holmes. "Munich was a red herring!"

Mycroft's eyebrows rose and descended in a figure eight of annoyance.

"A double red herring, if you please, sirs! I draw your attention to the item at the bottom of page one."

Our eyes dropped to scoop in the dread news. Moriarty's words had been no idle boast, and indeed his agents had been busy. However, the item had not been taken while its wearer slept, for the article detailed that the moustache was wired to a burglar alarm. That approach thwarted, the General had been set upon by ruffians and shaved.

Holmes and I turned to each other in terror.

"The moustache!" we said in unison.

"A most regrettable day for this fine nation of ours," said Mycroft solemnly, his back to us now. He surveyed the bustling metropolis outside with a sad eye.

"A terrible fate is to befall our small island nation, and these innocent souls go about their business as though all were well in the world. Ah, me."

His final sigh was a funeral bell within our bosoms. For a moment, there was no sound we were aware of, so great was the stake lost.

"I fear England is headed for war," said Holmes,

"Of course, that'll be nice," I said in hollow tribute to our proud military history.

"I fear events have undone us, gentleman," Mycroft intoned sadly as he turned from the window to face us. "The game is over, the final card played."

"It is unlike you, Mycroft, to concede defeat. Is their no clue, no lead?"

Mycroft ran his fingers along his shiny head, his face a mask of despair.

"I fear not. It was a clean job."

"No trace of any kind?"

"Just this big pile of monkey shit," said he, gesturing a side table. There upon a silver salver, in the club's best tradition, steamed the last hope for England.

"If you can draw anything from that, Sherlock, shovelled as it was from the scene, our dream of moustache driven supremacy need not be forgotten."

Stirred by this noble hope, Holmes produced two magnifying glasses from within his coat and, brandishing one in each hand, prepared to double fist his way to glory.

In the following several minutes, such a frenzy of detective action occurred as I have not seen in years. His zest, and zealous hope, led to a great effort. It was a speeded up effort of noble observation. Many of the club's members stood and applauded his sterling work.

Eventually the whirlwind was still. Standing at his full height once more, he looked up at us with a wary hope.

"I think I have the lead we require," said Holmes with a grim smile. "It may yet be too great a hope, but no avenue must be left unexplored."

Mycroft clapped a hand on his shoulder and pressed a note into his hand.

"The entire might of Britannia's proud forces are behind you, should you need them," said he with a tremor in his voice. "God speed!"

We left with the good wishes of all the club patrons, many of whom signalled their especial regard for Holmes' great powers by hurling buns at his head and shouting 'wanker.'

"There goes England's only hope," muttered one.

"We're fucked," said another, their chipper white moustaches quivering in patriotic fervour.

Outside the club, Holmes gestured to a policeman.

"We require an escort to the docks."

"Out for a bit of fun, are we, sir? With England in peril?" queried he, an air of disapproval about him.

Holmes bristled. Without uttering a word, he handed the policeman the note Mycroft had given him, to assure official co-operation.

The policeman read it quickly, then passed it back to Holmes. It read "My brother is a fool, however the situation is desperate. Please assist him all you can. Lend him no money."

Aware of Holmes' mounting chagrin, I beckoned to Inspector Gregson, who had been waiting outside for plot developments. I was explaining the situation to him when Holmes put in his two-penn'orth.

"Clearly we must race to the docks. If Moriarty's game is what I think, then he will need passage for himself and a monkey out of the country, post haste."

"The docks it is," said splendid Gregson, flagging a passing police wagon and ushering us into the back.

It was a tense ride as we raced along the highways that night. Knowing that England could be plunged into certain war, and that Holmes' much spattered reputation could ill afford yet further tarnishing, my stomach was knotted.

After a seeming eternity we arrived at our destination. Holmes raced out of the carriage, his every sense agog, aquiline hooter pulsating with the sea air and heady scent of clues.

We all stood for a time, taking in the rich and diverse sight of passengers and crew attending their business. Many of the richer patrons rested their weary frames on well-stuffed butlers; poorer fellows stared moodily at the pavement as the ship pulled into port.

I felt a tense tug at my elbow. Turning inquisitively to my colleague, I saw that he was gaping at a staggering sight, clearly too absorbed to explain himself.

Following his eye line, I too fell into a state of near shock (we were both too reserved and Victorian to fall into the real thing).

There, stood coolly in line with the other passengers, was Professor Moriarty, that damned soul of wretched perdition. He looked relaxed and ready for a holiday. His trousers were rolled up, there was a bucket and spade by his feet and that vast hairless noodle of his was covered by a
knotted hanky.

It was not that which held our fascination, however. Under his arm, tucked as casually as any umbrella, was a giant, moustache shaped package.

This was not the sole object of interest in the scene.

A small monkey crouched by his side, content with his simian pleasures of goosing old ladies and making 'bare it' gestures with his mouth.

"That's the man, Inspector. Use all excessive force possible," urged Holmes with a deep measure of satisfaction.

Inspector Gregson made good with his truncheon, whacking Moriarty several times squarely on the bonce and even giving him a cheeky tickle in the seat of his pants.

The stricken fiend clutched at his de-hankied coconut and let out several deeply satisfying cries of mega villain distress.

Holmes and I watched with many a chuckle, robustly enjoying this most satisfying end to yet another mystery.

"I feel the trousers of London will sleep sounder tonight for the knowledge that this arch fiend is safe behind bars."

And with that we turned, tripped and ate pavement.

"Great Scott, Holmes," said Mycroft some little time later. We were once more ensconced at his club. Mycroft had greeted us with great pride and vigour, generously announcing the drinks were on him.

He swirled his brandy luxuriously in its fine balloon glass while Holmes and I shared an orange juice. It was not the grandest of post case celebrations, however a deeply deserved one.

"I can hardly believe it," said he after a moment more of rumination. "Devil Moriarty hired a monkey trained to drop people's trousers. Using this as a screen, he secretly had designs on Sir-General Maving-Maving's moustache, which he planned to sell on the continent to the highest bidder."

"And upon seeing his master apprehended, this rogue chimp had one last reign of debagging terror."

Holmes smiled indulgently.

"Yes, the monkey went ape shit."

"Well, it would, wouldn't it, Holmes?" commented Mycroft reasonably. "And how ironic to think that is how you stumbled upon the conclusion to this whole dread matter."

"It is indeed, Mycroft. And now London can wake to a safer dawn, a dawn free from lowered pants, from a sleep no longer troubled by the knowledge that England's finest fighting facial hair is in danger."

Mycroft leaned over toward me in a conspiratorial manner.

"Does he always talk this much bollocks?"

"Always," I replied with a moody swig of orange. "Always."

"Damn! We've forgotten the women again!"

"Mine is this big!"

Even with the banana up his arse, Moriarty was still capable of wreaking havoc.

The Experience of the Quickest Client

I had rarely seen my friend in finer spirits than during the year '97. My highly selective accounts of his adventures had made him famous, and this heady fame brought Holmes a long roster of clients. It would be onerous for me to list all the great and the good who sought Holmes' advice, and I should be guilty of unpardonable indiscretion if I mentioned the illustrious names of some of his more famous clients. Suffice it to say I didn't vote for the Prime Minister again.

In this significant year a vast and impressive collection of cases caught Holmes' attention, reaching from his notorious investigation of the sudden death of Monsignor Rocheford – an enquiry that was carried out by him despite the express wishes of the Pope – down to his apprehension of Turner, the Bosun Street canary gobbler.

This success brought a greater measure of material comfort than we had been accustomed to. Holmes, however, lived for his art, and rarely accepted vast commissions on a Tuesday. Indeed it was on this day the portal outside 221b Baker Street had the 'closed' sign prominently displayed, although sometimes cases were still taken due to unusual circumstances.

As such, I was busier than ever chronicling the cases of my famous friend and keeping a record of his successes, which didn't take long. When work did not interfere, we spent our day of rest snoozing over the papers or, in Holmes' case, pretending to write learned monographs on some obscure subject. 'The final word,' my arse.

It was on such a Tuesday when the bell rang. Holmes raised his eyes impatiently at this intrusion, and from downstairs we could hear Mrs Hudson hefting around gold coins with subtle cries of "Whoopee!"

Some moments later an impeccably dressed figure appeared in our doorway. He had the bland, characterless eyes of a plutocrat. The gold fob watch sticking out of his pocket boasted of wealth so fabulous he tipped over to one side. Having taken in the room with a snooty glance, he sniffed and turned his face slightly. Clearly his expectations hadn't been met, and those hadn't been high.

Haughtily refusing to ever compromise his elite stature, Holmes raced out of his chair and bowed most low, twiddling every finger on his right hand as it swept before him, his left deftly extracting a thick wedge of notes from our client's pocket.

"My name is Simmondsley Welton, one of the Shropshire Weltons," he uttered with weary languor, pretending not to notice Holmes' larceny, a sign of true breeding. "We are all fabulously wealthy. I myself pass the time drinking champagne out of a grand piano; one piano per bottle, then they must be thrown away as it affects the tuning. In summer I get through four pianos a day."

"And I am Sherlock Holmes, your most elaborately humble servant. The man pawing at your feet with puppy dog eyes and waving a cap is Dr Watson. You may speak before him with absolute candour, because he usually misses everything."

"Absolutely."

Our visitor's cut glass vowels could have sawn the table in half. Unbidden, he made his way to the chez longue, upon which he draped himself with a malaise so stupendous Holmes was but an amateur in comparison. He himself had made a point of padding our client's footsteps with his fawning self, lest our visitor's shoe leather should be dirtied by the carpet.

"I shall begin, gentlemen, by emphasising the private nature of what I am about to tell you."

"You may speak with absolute confidence," assured Holmes.

"I will hold you to that, sir, as you are a gentleman–" here he broke off to look at me, under the mistaken impression I had sniggered, "–as the matter for me to relate is not for the common man to hear.

"It is an extraordinary tale I have to tell, sirs. Only last week I was visiting Surrey in order to give my land keepers instructions to irrigate the peasants. My business proved uneventful, although the peasants duly flooded.

"I made a stopover in London, wishing to mark my great Uncle Sebastian's birthday by bestowing upon him a gift of an engraved boncepiece."

"A fitting and gracious response," observed Holmes cautiously.

Our visitor preened knowingly.

"On my way to Uncle Sebastian's extensive studio flat in Whitehall and Westminster, I was lingering at a news stand, when I became engaged in conversation with the most dazzling fellow.

"I was – smitten, with this stranger. He had, apparently, written an important monograph on the subject of champagne corrosion in grand pianos. I am told that experts consider it the final word."

I resisted the temptation to make animal noises and start rending the furnishings with my teeth, but merely resumed listening with a patient, concerned face.

"We agreed to pursue our discussion later, when my appointment had been completed. He left me with his card, which I, alas, carelessly dropped."

Holmes, with his lungs finely attuned by smoking, inhaled. The wind scythed as he breathed in.

"Have you contacted me merely to resume a conversation?" queried he, near timorous at the prospect of such a wretched development.

"Indeed. What of it?" he enquired, imperiously flinging fivers at Holmes.

"Oh nothing, nothing," purred Holmes, gazing in wonder at the opulent confetti flittering before his eyes.

I was unsure of quite what to think of this client. That said, I was most certain of how to behave. I knelt tartly before him and applied coat after coat of lickspittle shoe polish to his already gleaming spats. He in turn graciously consented to rest his teacup on my head, and as such we became the best of friends.

Holmes too, I could tell, was unsure on how best to advise our auspicious guest. So far he had confined himself to merely looking outraged and defiant, as is his wont when dealing with wealthier persons, but now his expression wore a dazed countenance.

"I know him only as D." Our foppish guest sniffed. "I should very much like to know who he is."

With that he hurled another sprinkling of money into the air and departed, leaving Holmes nonplussed and me with a tea-stained forehead.

It was a welcome diversion from our domestic life of late. We had been cursed with a visit from Holmes' Uncle Doris, a very eccentric man with most peculiar tastes.

Upon the instructions of this unusual guest, our housekeeper Mrs Hudson had been slicing the carrots into penis shapes and making little broccoli balls, after the syphilitic poet, Byron.

In fact, all our meals now had a bizarre tackle theme. Even the toast was shaped like underpants.

This added little pleasure to our Baker Street dinners. Holmes and I would sit in great discomfort, chewing minimally and swallowing rarely, as outrage upon outrage was served before our bulging eyes. He even had an arse shaped gravy boat.

Doris, on the other hand, loved it, and downed the lot with an odious smacking of his lips. He would hail us to lower our reservations and join in, as we would 'obviously love it,' if we could only unbuckle our reservations.

A dreadful time. When I peruse my notes appertaining to this period I can only find a series of shudders, which are very difficult to spell.

During the consultation he had been attending to his toilet, which he polished assiduously. He now entered the sitting room, waving a toothbrush cheerfully.

I looked at the instrument with loathing. The more learned of my readers will know that brushing the teeth causes corrosions of the fangs, and is considered a most unwise move for those wanting sound gnashers and a disease free head.

Myself, I could hold nothing with such eccentric, not to say dangerous practices. My own teeth have never been brushed, not once in their lives. Instead every morning and evening I swill with imperial strength bath polish, relying upon that to keep my mouth clean in more ways than one. This was a truism I knew for a fact because now when I say 'turd,' it sparkles.

Holmes was with me on this matter. He sat before the mantel, contemplating the matter with a distant gaze as he sifted through a big roll of fivers.

He sneezed and deposited several teeth into his handkerchief.

"Watson, I believe I have it. Ah, Doris," said he, upon noticing our guest's presence. "You missed a most interesting visit. A gentleman of limitless means and pleasing aspect."

"Say on," purred our guest. Holmes and I covered our willies and looked away.

With a sudden knock the door flew open, and there once more stood our mysterious visitor.

"Forgive my reappearance with so little fanfare," he nodded curtly in our direction.

Before he had finished even that small sentence, Holmes was fawning in attendance, slippers between his teeth and pooch like hands flopping meekly before him. He could not have been better disciplined as our natural social better balanced a biscuit on his aquiline nose and waved cash at him until he was allowed to eat it.

Having finished his delightful reintroduction, he busied himself paving a way to the sofa with Van Goghs.

Uncle Doris gave a polite, slight but highly significant cough. Our visitor looked up and their eyes locked like horny giraffes.

The two lovers squealed enthusiastically.

"Doris!"

"Fuzzycock!"

They rushed into each other's arms and smooched with a ferocity that singed the curtains, then disappeared together.

For a moment all between us was surprise, then Holmes smirked knowingly, the complacent expression on his face no match for the complete mask of confusion on his features.

"I knew it from the very first," he pronounced in his most laconic, complacent drawl.

"Cobblers!" said I, and struck him unconscious with a mallet.

"I know it's a bit early in the day to ask Dolly for head, but ..."

Holmes and I were both great fans of Clint Eastwood.

"… and here's where I catch the bad guy. Ah, I love that bit!"

The Conundrum of the Missing Motherfucker

I was glancing over my notebooks recently when it occurred to me that the followers of my celebrated friend's career would never forgive me if I did not mention one of the few occasions when Mr Sherlock Holmes' much admired talents were unequal to the task facing him.

It was a dull January in 1902 when the bizarre events in question began to unfold. They brought such darkness to the crevices of criminal London that the entire capital appeared to sicken under the miasma of some debilitating virus.

Wherever the innocent citizen walked smears of snotty crime flecked the pavements. I myself was inconvenienced on a number of instances after tripping over the victims of street robbery, and on one particularly sad occasion dropped an almost full bag of toffee.

Returning to my perpetual home of 221b Baker Street, my dear wife having moved me out of my consulting rooms in order to built a gym for Scandinavian athletes, I tossed my hat Bond style onto the hat stand and greeted Mrs Hudson.

"Good day, dear housekeeper."

"Get stuffed, fat doctor. I'm cleaning and that ponce detective is doing his dying swan impression upstairs."

"Great Scott!" I cried in some alarm, distressed by this news. Holmes was renowned for his complete inability to face everyday life rationally. This is part of what made him great, for some reason. Certainly without his singular and extraordinary skills even the very few people who found him tolerable would have dismissed him as a complete arse years ago. I was still tempted to do so on occasion.

However, I found the news of Holmes' condition most alarming. I was afraid he may have ingested some substance of which it is unwise for anyone of his farty constitution to imbibe. The possibility of a relapse into his habitual addictions – cocaine, excessive amounts of tweed and an overdependence on pencil drawings among the narration – was calamitous.

I had spent the greater part of the previous year strongly encouraging him to eat mints whenever the urge to get blitzed off his pasty face with drugs struck him. I had been largely unsuccessful in this endeavour, although his behaviour while fucked up had improved. He no longer played the violin while wasted, preferring to make syncopated jazz noises by tapping his spare magnifying glasses together.

I ran to Holmes' room where, much as I feared, a sight of narcotic indulgence met my eye. Holmes was sprawled over the floor, his shirtsleeves rolled up tightly at the elbow and a series of injection marks told their sad tale.

"Holmes!" I cried and gathered his head from the floor.

"Ow, you bastard!" said he, opening one bloodshot eye long enough to send me a look of peculiar distaste. His noble countenance was animated by what appeared to be a strong desire to biff me over the head with any nearby ornament.

"Holmes, what is this? Why have you returned to your nefarious relaxants? Is the detective work not satisfying you?" I was aghast at my friend's condition, and concerned that he may permanently damage the unique talents which had made his name.

He chuckled softly to himself and slowly rose from the floor.

"Ah, poor Watson!" said he, after furnishing himself with his pipe and holding a match to the bowl. "I had forgotten how much these indulgences of mine worry the professional in you." He appeared far more his old commanding self, and I was cheered greatly by this demonstration that reason was returning to her throne.

I assisted Holmes in finding his way to an armchair - not a task that I would have thought would be very taxing for a detective, as there were six of them in the room - and watched as he began to recover his regular demeanour.

After he had sat up long enough, imbibing a cup of tea and eating a sandwich, I broached the question which had caused me such great vexation.

"What means this return to your narcotics, Holmes?" I enquired. It is true that I am far from equipped to appreciate the malaise which affects his temperament; however I do like to know what is going through his mind. For one thing, it is usually a sound indicator of how much toilet paper is required.

"Fear not, old friend," he replied with a twinkle in his eye. "It is not my intention to regularly imbibe the old seven percent cocaine solution which, I fear, has occasioned you a certain amount of worry in the past." He chuckled quietly to himself as he said this, leading me to conclude that perhaps his regret was rather less than he made out.

"Rest assured that when the criminal element of this city present me with a task worthy of my talents, I will find no more need for distraction than the busiest of bees. I take it you have seen the newspapers?"

I poured myself a steaming cup, relishing even the briefest of returns to his old form. Holmes discussing crime, even when impishly mourning the absence of ingenuity on those occasions when the expert in him was greater than the citizen, was not a man devoid of interest.

I replied I had not seen anything of great note in the news.

"Precisely!" said he, a glint of triumph clear in his eye. "There is not the smallest matter of note in any of these sad, tawdry affairs." He sprawled luxuriously in the great chair and airily gestured towards the side table holding the illustrated dailies.

"The plainest of eyes can detect a city weighted under the indolent glaze of boredom. Even the most vicious of brazen assaults is conducted with the resignation of a dissatisfied bank clerk. One report from the annals of yesterday's street robbery said that the brazen gunman was seen stifling a yawn as he prodded at his victim with a revolver. We live in decadent times!"

With this he rose abruptly to his feet, turning to face the window with an imperiousness that was less of an angry gesture and more of a flounce.

Piqued by my colleague's unsociable mood, accustomed though I was to his irrationality, I angrily snatched up the uppermost newspaper and affixed it with an intense, moody stare. Skipping straight to the cartoons, I spent the next quarter hour familiarising myself with the ongoing difficulties of seducing a woman who keeps punching you, with comically exaggerated effect, in the teeth.

What is love? I thought to myself, and my mind flit back to golden days of summers gone by, when I, a newly qualified military doctor with a commission for The King's Own Anachronisms, thought myself a most dapper fellow, with my then rather svelte 44 inch waistline, newly acquired uniform of stiff shapeless green cardboard and freshly polished head.

Fellows graduating from my Alma Mater, the distinguished Dr Crippen Centre for Military Medicine, traditionally descended upon London society toward the end of the social season. At this time, the more eligible young ladies had already bucked their wild horses.

Fellow graduates and myself confined ourselves to descending on Bingford Hall and romancing the local ladies by having embarrassment competitions in the their gardens. This was helped by the many statues of men with gigantic funsacks.

Thoughts of these halcyon days worked through my system like a powerful laxative intended for stuffed up elephants. I shuddered and resumed my perusal of The Thrilling Mysteries Of Richard 'The Human Revolver' Ackroyd; a daredevil of a man who has wrestled more tigers, ignored more local customs and drunk more gin than any other in the British Empire.

This superhuman fellow had recently been toasted as the finest of Englishmen; a man of wit and honour, with an eye for justice and a quick hand for dispensing lead. Thrilling as I was to his bold deeds as expertly told by his biographer, the redoubtable Arthur Bagglington-Snorke, late of the Africa Corps of the Army and Navy Stores, the day began to look well.

A loud, pained snort erupted from Holmes' direction. I gathered that my celebrated flatmate had observed what I was reading and expressed his disdain. Upon discovering that his own 'trifling' publications had a rival; a younger, fitter one at that, with a bigger brain and fuller underpants, had thrown Holmes into self-important despair. Having been used for so many years to being the only crime specialist in the world, which was bullshit at the best of times, Holmes had taken this rather hard. Perhaps it was this, and not indolence driven malaise, which heralded a return to his narcotic interests.

I attempted to resume my study of the thrilling adventures which lay before me in page form, but the impacting buffet of a well-aimed magnifying glass interrupted my enjoyment. Smiling at Holmes in a wan fashion, I reached for my hat and the stick which acted as a bum deterrent, and headed outdoors.

Sauntering toward my regular haunts was no small pleasure for me, as I had been confined indoors of late with a mild but persistent head cold. My constitution having never fully recovered after my exertions serving the Empire in the far East, I had of late considered it most prudent to remain indoors and catalogue my lingerie collection. Now that I felt my strength fully returned, hastened no doubt by Holmes' most recent descent into adolescence, I was robustly enjoying my perambulation.

I headed straight for my club, The Stout Sidekick, and commandeered the finest armchair in the establishment. Settled in the heart of London's premier second fiddle establishment, I ordered the most potent drink on the menu. This was the daunting, liver mangling Arsebuster Supreme, which, comprising as it does equal measures of port, cider, turpentine and cranberry juice, remains the finest means of knackering sobriety known to this medical professional.

I passed a most enjoyable afternoon imbibing several of these with the daily papers. I feel it is true to say that not a very large amount of time had gone by before the newsprint became but an indecipherable blur before my hazy eyes. I dozed happily beneath a cover of broad sheeted bigotry and dreamed of giant foreign powers hiding my willy.

It was some hours later when I rose and, pausing for a moment to steady my uncertain legs, headed on my way home. The route from The Stout Sidekick to Baker Street takes in Booley Road, which houses Finnerans, the largest, plushest bookshop in the country. Many years ago it was my modest practice to visit Finnerans once upon a fortnight, for the purposes of doffing my hat to unescorted ladies and sandwiching my wang between the pages of romance novels.

Feeling a passing toot of nostalgia for those idyllic days of yore, I headed once again through the hallowed literary portals which had seen more of my plonker than any bookshop has a right. Again I marvelled at the fine arrays of literary wealth stacked neatly on the magnificent shelves. I had selected a volume of Mr Cecil Jeremy's Tweaking Tips to peruse when my attention was arrested by the whisper of a distant voice.

"... unt so from zis recollection ve can determine zat zis vee fellow, who is clearly in a state of vot ve call trouser denial, vazzed in the vater glass und in ze

144

process traumatising poor Dora, solely because on zat von occasion ven he vas a youth, he vas unable to piss higher zan his friend Sebastian."

A smattering of polite applause followed this bizarre speech. For a moment I was completely distracted, and neglected to pay attention to where I was walking.

The unexpected thunder of twenty-two stone of doctor colliding with barely five ounces of small bony assistant split the bookstore's quiet reverence. In a bluster of confusion and disarray I found my balance compromised. I stumbled everywhere.

There was a moment of blur, and what appeared to be a blizzard of pages descending upon me. All was confusion for a moment. Soon, my hat had been restored and the straps reapplied to various quadrants of girth. I steadied my substantial personage under the neat tuckings of my Poggs and St. John's Son waistcoat.

The narrow gentleman I had flattened was being pried out of the floorboards. Awkwardly, I attempted to adjust my manner to this unexpected turn of events. I cleared my throat and wrung my hands.

I am sorry to report that this remorseful behaviour did not calm the matter down. Far from it, there now appeared to be around four thousand gawping parties staring with shock or glee at my difficult predicament. Things had got so bad I even wished Holmes was here to assist. Suffice it to say that I was very baldly in the full glare of public attention.

Mr Twattlington, the proprietor, greeted me with euphoric cries of "Get out, you fat perv." I turned with a delighted smile on my lips ready to greet this old friend. Indeed he was exactly as I remember, even pointing me out to Charles the oversized doorman and making the same 'crush them' gestures of old while pointing at my nuts.

On a more regular day I would have waved cheerily, but the words filtering through from the adjourning room diverted my attention once again. As such I barely noticed the two vast gentlemen with the half chewed ears descending upon me. Feeling that a note or two of currency would benefit me considerably, I felt into my pocket for my notecase.

Finding only the butt of my revolver, I recollected how I had not emptied said firearm from my overcoat after Holmes' last great adventure, The Mystery of the Misplaced Knacker. Filled with nostalgia and briefly distracted as I was, my fingers fumbled with the pistol, which discharged itself with a cordite bellow that shook the room like the last fart during a papal funeral.

The effect upon the shop was electric. My bullet had scarce finished pinging off the cash register and embedding itself safely into the head of a passing beggar when I realised with some embarrassment that all eyes were on me.

"I'm sorry," I murmured earnestly. "I didn't mean to alarm anyone, but my gun went off accidentally."

A great quacking guffaw emerged from the other room, from where the lecturer's enticing voice had been heard earlier. Suddenly several hundred pairs of bulging eyes were fixed upon me. Their owners were all crammed breathlessly into the doorway and watching me, a crowd hotly expecting to witness a rare treat.

The two fearsome employees, only a moment again so plainly hellbent on wrecking my fine face with the epitome of all smashings, had backed away to the point. They were now attempting to blend in with the furniture. Their nefarious commander Mr Twattlington had experienced a similar reversal in mood, and was now attempting to meekly hide his circumferential physique behind a pencil.

I covered the difficult moment as best I could, waving away the clouds of gunpowder emanating from my singed overcoat and inadvertently grabbed a passing lady.

"Oh my great good heavens," I murmured in mortified atonement. "How dreadful of me! You must

146

think I am Jack the Ripper's more savage elder brother. Pray conceal your difficult emotions behind my trousers," I offered helpfully, and was in the process of removing said garment when the poor woman slipped into a heavy faint, landing on a section marked Light Romance, which she had neatly squashed into a dense, envelope sized pile of debris.

I absolved myself immediately of all responsibility as she was less well dressed than I. Clearly I was the victim, and the disgraceful harridan who assaulted me one of the vile dregs of London's underworld. I disregarded her employee badge, reading "Hi, I'm Shirley, can I help?", and prepared to evacuate my bowels over the store to distract people.

"Sssh. Note how zis man attempts to blame zis poor female for his own clumsiness."

I was thunderstruck and astounded by this distinctly un-English way of approaching the matter. Surely anyone who was even half a gentleman would join in my excoriation of the poor woman and save my bloated self from further disgrace? Turning upon my heels, slowly, due to my advanced tonnage and delicate ankles, I faced the man who had spoken of me in this unusual fashion.

He was tall, intelligent looking man. I remember thinking he was probably an academic, not because of his intelligent face but due to the threadbare state of his clothing. Even his bald patch looked second hand. He adjusted his spectacles and a pallid fluttering of intellect stirred behind his eyes.

"Fascinating!" said he from behind about eight feet of shrubbery. I attempted to begin rescrutinising him, but in his manner was a detached observation the level of which I had only seen in Holmes, and only then while pouring over his credit card statement.

"I see you are uncomfortable in public," said he pleasantly. The calm in his voice suggested he knew nothing, or cared nothing, of the burning Victorian guilt which lurked beneath my fractured, torpid manner.

"I see from ze narration above that you have become somevot rattled, Herr Doctor. Also, you are single? Perhaps you vould benefit from a long path of ass gazing therapy?"

My palms were sweaty, tight and tense as I ran them heavily over my already sodden trousers. Working hard to sound confident, I blustered my best.

"I think you'll find that I cut quite a dash with the ladies," I said, trying hard to conjure images of myself tripping the light fantastic with a succession of adoring beauties, none of whom looked like my mother.

This only served to draw a rich, well tobaccooed chuckle out of him. Wondering if now was the time to put my red face to the test by making some chin music, I moved a little further to my strange antagonist.

Instead of backing away or raising bunches of five for a little pop-pop Queensbury style, he twirled one side of his moustache. Leaning his weight back onto his dapper feet, he laid a hand on my shoulder. Flummoxed by his unusual way of dealing with this situation, I could only be swayed by his persuasive manner.

"I think you and I need a talk, my glowing sprinkler system of a friend."

The days that followed my talk with Dr Freud are still a whirl in my mind. It is true that I considered myself quite a ladies man, having paid for sex in several countries and once even having got it free. But this kind and patient Viennan showed me a world of trouser related intrigue which not even an experienced military gentleman such as myself could have predicted.

Following the close of our conversation, I decided that my life would be greatly different. I would throw off the shackles of our repressive Victorian society (or at least, I would throw them off as far as I could without exciting comment) and live a purer, more natural and robustly fulfilled life.

In the weeks that passed after this meeting, my life gained and became far richer than I had ever known. I stopped sandpapering my genitals prior to bedtime, instead avoiding the dreaded 'nightime milkshake' that sleep can bring by gluing together the end of my thigh tickler. I felt far more in touch with myself for this, and not in the way that requires lengthy jail time or a merciful bullet.

Considering Dr Freud's views on the importance of a healthy subconscious, I laid out photographs of all my relatives and walked around naked in front of them, imagining fondly to myself how they may react to such conduct. My great Aunt Maude, who once immolated a man for disgracefully allowing his socks to slip down and show his ankles, would most definitely have been bellowing for her elephant gun.

Naturally, I did this in absolute, disgraced privacy. I would mutter a few distracted words in passing to either Holmes or Mrs Hudson, and proceed straight to locking myself in my room and continue parading nuts out before the gallery of my constipated looking forebears.

Deprived of my gormless companionship, Holmes fell into a foul and petulant temper. He kicked the cat so often the poor thing looked sore and walked with an exaggerated limp, and had taken to giving all and sundry the most hurt looks of resentment.

It was rare that I saw my distinguished colleague in such a poor mood. Following my illuminating discussion with Dr Freud there descended upon him a miffedness, a miffedness which was almost without parallel in my experience of his temperament. In fact, when the patented Holmes' mood chartometre in my room, I saw that he was currently on a Stupendous Huff. The line was hovering worryingly close to Substantial Malaise and only three pissed off notches below the dreaded Torrential Fipsy.

This dreaded and vaporous attack of hubristic malaise descended on him only when the rarest of snooterings had occurred. One such incident was the time he discovered Professor Moriarty had given him the slip during the great Victoria Line adventure by getting off at a different station.

A variety of things could explain his current foul temper. One might be the slow development of plot, a thing always guaranteed to rouse his slumbering inner bitch. Also his torrentially foul mood downpour could be connected with my hiring a slinky new assistant to help with my onerous task of chronicling Holmes' sterling adventures.

She was a fine asset and certainly not difficult to look at. I had acquired her, at great expense incurred by one of Holmes' wealthier clients, from the esteemed Curves Agency, run by the inestimable Madam Curves, one of London's more respectable madams.

Said nubile secretary had finished rearranging my increasingly sparse comb over and moved off my lap with a saucy kissy-kiss gesture and a wiggle.

"Well done, Miss Bellamy!" I said with an approval of such deep relish I could taste it in my moustache. Life, I felt, had taken a considerable step for the better.

The following morning both Holmes and I could be found about our business at an exceptionally early time. In fact, I had just fished a cigarette end out of my boiled egg when it occurred to me that Mrs Hudson fixing the breakfast directly upon returning after Ladies' Night at the Pig & Felcher was not the best idea. On these occasions she habitually returns with the milk, often hurling said bottle of mine or Holmes' window in a genial expression of goodwill.

"Holmes, we really must speak to Mrs Hudson. These habits of hers have become deplorable. Only last week I found her using my trousers to go ferreting."

Holmes cocked a spare eyebrow.

"Indeed, Watson? Did she catch anything?"

"Not a single ferret."

"You surprise me. I should have thought that, with her somewhat individual approach her bag would have been filled most easily!"

Holmes was alluding to Mrs Hudson's known practice of leaving a tray of sandwiches out in the open and hovering above, clutching a rope with a knife between her teeth. Many innocent ferrets had met their end at Mrs H.'s hands; presumably their last moments were a mixture of glee at the prospect of sandwiches and terror at having our housekeeper land on them brandishing a knife.

His eyes narrowed at my words, and I knew he was once more devoting a portion of his immense brain to the resolution of this trivial, domestic matter. Holmes rarely had any time for matters outside his professional field, and so I suspected he was deriving far more from this situation than would meet the casual eye.

"Watson, I fancy the way our dear housekeeper approaches rodents is not unlike the fashion after which a criminal predator pursues his mark." Holmes swept his arm over the table, palms up, and accidentally sent cornflakes all over the place.

"Very true, Holmes," I said, pacifying him. It was not my intention nor my place to provoke further spiritual malaise in Holmes by telling me he was talking utter wank. In truth I was heartened and relieved to find him almost his old self again, and not the miserable curmudgeon who had been doing the cat such damage of late with his self-indulgent tossery.

I was spooning another dollop of cornflakes into the face when a tremendous knocking could be heard from downstairs. The effect on my colleague was extraordinary.

"Haha, Watson!" said he with great relish, leaping out of his seat and thumping an effusive hand upon my napkined knee. "If I am not much mistaken, that knock heralds the arrival of the plot. If you see Mrs Hudson, have her bring it in!" His voice had risen into that near falsetto pitch of the deranged artisan that lived within his frail, overused temples.

In due and short course an embossed envelope arrived on a silver salver, next to a freshly bottled turd, one of Mrs Hudson's regrettable lapses into sordid humour which could make our time at 221B Baker Street something of a trial.

Holmes leaned forward and picked up the proffered telegram. He held it close before his eyes, perusing with that intense detail for which he is so widely celebrated. For a brief instant he appeared almost vacant, such was the intensity of his concentration. The famed aquiline nose fluttered slightly as he held the expensive blue paper taut beneath his nostrils, eyes narrowed while he appeared to grope the air for detail.

"Intriguing," he murmured, a dreamy expression passing over his face while his cogitative machinery whipped itself into high gear. "Smell that, Watson," he invited. Wondering if he had just cracked off a sly one, and preparing to take steps, I warily made my way over. Holmes merely held out the telegram.

"Notice you anything?"

I held the paper before my nose and took in a good whiff. My nostrils picked up a rich melange of sense tinglers; ale, cologne, bicycle leather and linseed oil. An intriguing concoction.

I voiced my conclusions to Holmes, and he nodded in agreement.

"Whoever sent this is setting me a challenge."

For a moment I was tempted to mutter my agreement, but then I was seized by a brainwave.

"I know, Holmes. Why not read it?"

His face lit up.

"Watson, you excel yourself! Hand it over."

I passed forward the telegram in question and Holmes quickly scanned it for meaning, then turned it over and read the side with the writing on it.

Whatever the contents, they drew a richly satisfied chuckle from my colleague. I was relieved to see that he appeared to be more than ever his old self.

"It would seem that my services are required at the highest level, Watson. A matter of delicacy, I gather, and an issue of grave regard is at stake."

He passed the telegram forward to me once again. I took it and, instead of smelling it, this time read the type.

'Send four bunches of finest tulips to the usual fellow who cares nothing for sprouts. Be sure tell nobody what you do. Heads that roll will roll south. The well fed pigeon enjoys only mayonnaise.'

"Christ, what a load of shit!" was all I could think of to say.

Holmes winced, and I regretted my outburst directly I saw his face. He, being of sensitive (twatty) disposition, must be handled with the rare delicacy that one may afford a Ming vase.

Holmes made to reply, evidently whirling himself into a wind of suffering indignation. I wondered for a brief moment how many people who blessed to share a flat with both a dedicated scientist and a delicate artisan. Putting one of my patented stalling tactics into play, I feigned distraction.

"Christ, what a load of shit gets written in these damn horoscopes," I blustered, waving a page or two of newsprint to lend credence to my bluff. "I'm sorry, Holmes. The telegram, we were talking about the telegram, yes? Well, it's either a fiendishly devised bit of code or else an elaborate bluff. Saving, of course, the possibility that your correspondent is a drooling fruit basket."

Holmes' acuity and sharp antennae had, like all that rare man's gifts, the blind spot of his vanity. Fresh from my perusal of my own life through the graceful intellect of Dr Freud, I was also mindful of another trapdoor into Holmes' psychology, and this one less thoroughly mined.

Nonchalantly, I reached into my breast pocket and produced a pair of Miss Bellamy's fragrant undergarments, which I used to mop the perspiration which had gathered on my forehead.

Holmes could only stare, stammer and foam a little at the mouth. Safe in the knowledge that I had been the victor in our little exchange, I waited gracefully for him to gather all his detecting kit. Minute after minute ticked by as he gathered magnifying glasses, vials of rare chemicals, his revolver and so forth. Eventually he appeared ready, anticipation written all over his face.

"My assignation," Holmes informed me as we made our way, "is with one of the highest level and most secretive of all agents in Europe. He has acted for many of Europe's greatest families, and his knowledge of encryption and enigma are second to none."

"Why are you meeting him, then?" I asked, feeling that this paragon would do far better, whatever the situation, without my erstwhile colleague's at times blithering efforts.

"It seems there are security concerns with the safety of a well renown man, whose intellect is reputedly among the finest in the world. It will be pleasant, indeed, to have some company whose intellect is the equal of my own."

I waited until Holmes was distracted and then pulled the most miffed face in my repertoire of expressions. The scoundrel! I made a mental note to include some unpleasant details about Holmes in the narrative later on, then let him continue with the matter at hand.

I consider myself a proud man, but above the simple pettiness that allows such things to rankle. As such, I completed my toilet with a quiet dignity that became me well, humming gently and bottling a fart in Holmes' favourite aftershave bottle.

Chuckling quietly to myself and donning my hat, I descended the stairs quickly, adopting my most serious expression as I entered the carriage and took my place beside Holmes. He had adopted a theatrical pose, sitting rigidly upright with his hands resting discreetly on his lap.

The journey was brief but intense. The incessant trundling of the wheels added a frisson of expectation and pace to our enquiry. A short while later we were outside a prominent London landmark which, out of respect for Holmes' professional discretion, I will not name. I will say that Nelson was looking particularly well, although the pigeons still have no respect for England's naval heroes.

Holmes' contact was an exotic looking man, a tall figure in a perfectly tailored coat. He had been standing with an air of detached nonchalance when our carriage pulled up. Casually folding his newspaper he walked, with studied nonchalance, to the side where Holmes alighted.

Expressionless they faced each other, both with a sombre tint visible within their richly textured eyes. The contact began the ritual first.

"The well fed pigeon finds the mayonnaise not to his taste and has decided upon tomato soup."

"He would be well advised to avoid inferior brands."

"To speak carelessly of Schubert is to invite ridicule."

"Only from three part movers."

"It takes a bold move to outwit the sage of Wigan."

"May his enemies find their comeuppance ripe."

A beat passed quickly as the bizarre ritual ended with lavish wishes of mutual goodwill. I gathered Holmes and this man had a rich history of adventures and shared intrigue between them. In the simplest of gestures – the clasp of a hand, the significance of a word – an implicit bond of trust and fellowship was established.

Our contact led us from the sooty bosom of criminal London's foetid alleyways to the lobby of the swankiest hotel in our capital, the French influenced Hotel Brenleur. Many finely attired guests were having a graceful bite to eat at the exclusive Manger aux Merde grill, and Holmes passed them with the characteristic hauteur of a man who cannot afford the prices.

Dextrously pocketing a tomato as we passed the diners, we made our way through and pretended to be lost so that I could fill my pockets with ketchup sachets while Holmes patiently inspected the menu through his 75 power magnifying glass, and tried to prevent himself from blanching with horror at the vast sums required to eat even the merest kipper.

To examine these luxurious trappings for signs of security flaws did seem a trifle ridiculous, as if the majority of major criminals could even afford the substantial tip the doorman would require to allow access. We eyed the patrons with a measure of suspicious envy, and swept past to meet our new client.

Our lavish host was waiting for us at the outer reception of his vast suite of rooms. Craning our heads as we did so to look past him, his set of posh rooms reached out further than the eye could see. I fancy I could even see a lagoon retreating into the distance, so great was this luxury, past the aviary stuffed with kestrels and the zoo next to the mini bar.

Stunned, we looked at the doctor with boggling eyes as he smiled at us with gracious welcome.

"Welcome to my humble rooms. Please forgive my less zan perfect grasp of English. I am a very busy man, and have had to learn your beautiful language by studying correspondence, reading letter upon letter ven I could find no-one vith voom to practice conversing. It is a painful matter to me zat your ears vill be sullied by a less than perfect grasp of your native tongue –"

"Oooee!" I thought to myself. "Now there's an eponymous slip!"

"– but at least I have been able to accept that it is not correct to end conversations with the words 'yours sincerely,' so there is at least that much to be thankful for."

Holmes nodded his gracious assent to our host's thoughtful words. My esteemed colleague prides himself on his courtly manners, as was in evidence here; for he waited until Dr Freud's back was turned before making the famous "I am a blithering monkey with shit for brains face" he generally reserves for members of Scotland Yard.

"It must be something of an interference for you to come und assess my humble safety needs."

Holmes demurred politely, never wanting to antagonise or belittle a rich patient. He waited quietly, and I could tell from that quiet manner of reserve that he was fervently gripping his gold money clip and dreaming of a diamond studded magnifying glass.

"I am sure you have read much on my new theory, zat of psychoanalysis and the way of reading people's inner thoughts through dream analysis."

"Oh yes," said Holmes, looking vacant but optimistic.

"I can tell you are a serious man. So I vill tell you zis, I am under no threat. It would make no sense, and besides, my security is ample," he said, waving his hand at a squad of attack elephants grazing attentively under one of the chandeliers.

"They have taken very gut care of me. So please, do try a snootful of this, Mister Holmes," he beckoned politely, proffering what I recognised at once as a syringe of medical grade Columbian nose tickler.

Holmes' eyes lit up with delight and he strode forward, rolling up a sleeve.

Perhaps it is better to glaze over this incident, an occasion which saw two giants in their field truly lowering themselves. The coked up pair went on a terrific voyage of intoxicated discovery, reducing a good deal of the furniture to its composite parts, soiling the curtains and, at one particularly wretched point, throwing the gramophone through the window.

I, as a non-imbiber of such dreadful medicine, merely sat quietly, watching the proceedings unfold as I sipped a cup of tea. It was difficult to appear unperturbed as this pair of headspun nutjobs tore about the flat, but I managed as best I could.

Some while later the gleeful madness subsided. The potent chemicals had worked most of their destructive magic and the ravages of dissipation had calmed their hellion moods.

As they parted, their pale strained faces were wrought with the physical effort of withstanding such stimulus. Holmes' eyes were as wan and red as I had ever seen, and Dr Freud's could be found somewhere within the deep recesses of his beard.

When some of the layers of shit had been hosed from the floor, and the stench of fossilised vein had largely abated, the two calmed and said their goodbyes.

"Thank you for your hospitality, Dr Freud. I commend you on your fine taste."

"Guten-bye, Mr Holmes. I will of course remain your most obvious servant."

Wavering slightly over this somewhat puzzling malapropism, we departed, myself rubbing my hands and braced afresh following this new encounter with the good doctor. Holmes, for his part, was far less content with the matter. As we left, he kept looking back over his shoulder, as if hoping to find some clue or hoover up a last grain of cocaine.

Instead, whenever he looked back he found the same courteous figure of Dr Freud, beaming and eyeing us with grave pleasure as we made our way out.

Over the days that followed our encounter, I found Holmes distracted. Once again his world became an immersion within a sphere that was the near kin of his soul. For days on end he laboriously sat up studying the intricacies of molecular chemistry. Bizarre plumes of odiferous smoke discharged themselves through the sitting room windows at all hours, and any wandering pedestrian strolling past our roof ran the serious risk of random incineration.

It was with heavy heart that I entered our flat that fateful Tuesday. My heart was heavy, as was my stomach, for I had just received terrible news after an immense lunch. I trudged wearily up the stairs, leaving many a deep footprint in the groaning timber. So vile was the news I had received, and so difficult to digest was the two ton urchin pie (made with real urchins), that I doubted I would be up for my scheduled despunking session with Miss Bellamy.

"Holmes, dreadful news," I began, starting my tale of dread woe as I entered the sitting room. "You won't believe this but ..." and my voice trailed off as a bizarre scene met my eyes.

Holmes was crouched naked over the sitting room table, his balls in the butter dish. Before him was a microscope which he peered into, his hunched shoulders and flared buttocks testimony to his extreme level of concentration. Before his screwed up eyeball was the lens of a powerful microscope, and clutched in a tense, bony hand was a scalpel.

"My dear fellow," I stammered. "I confess myself somewhat undone by this sight. What, in the name of all that is holy, are you doing?"

"Trying to split the atom."

I shook my head and took off my coat. With a sad motion towards this sorry mess, I regaled Holmes with my terrible news.

"Freud has been kidnapped. There have been police crawling all over his suite, trying to find drugs, money and the telephone numbers of some of his many conquests. They request your help at the most urgent level."

With that I leaned back into my chair and took a surprisingly hairy mouthful of buttered toast. My esteemed colleague looked at me thoughtfully, extracting his nuts from said dish and straightened his hair with a wan finger.

"I fancy, Watson, you have perhaps been plague to the vast flurrying mills of gossip that power many tongues in this fine city." He was now sat near motionless in the corner, a volume on the study of disappearing psychiatrists held within his slender grasp.

I begged him, for my sake, to stop being a twat and pull his finger out. The resulting mess I take full responsibility for.

We raced to the scene of the crime with all alacrity; once, that is, Holmes had stopped gut laughing at the unfortunate doctor's wretched fate. I myself was rather more concerned. The counsel I had received from this fine Viennan had been an epiphany, and I doubted the human race would ever truly recover from the loss of such a great mind, if indeed mortal peril lay in his path.

How very different it would be if Holmes' life were in the balance.

He had been the most peculiarly antagonistic company of late, and were it his life at risk – say, for example, if some moustachioed, top hatted villain tied him to a railway line – then I should not expend undue energy in racing to his aid. In fact, should such a situation occur, then I do believe I should probably saunter along at quite an idle pace, possibly stopping for a bite of lunch en route. I might even read a book as well; a railway timetable, perhaps.

We arrived at the Ritz Hotel, where the concerned crowds, agitated policemen and worried family members were all conspicuous by their absence. Realising we had directed our carriage to the wrong hotel, we dashed into the dining room for a quick meal – four courses, brandy and cigars – and then raced to the scene of the crime.

Freud's hotel was indeed whirled into a mighty state of commotion. Outside the lobby a thronging crowd had to be calmed by the Police Performing Arts Society reprising their triumphant staging of *The Vagina*

Monologues ("A triumph," Bristol Evening Post, "I wept and howled," Tavistock Gazette).

Recognising the dangerous mood of the everyday London dwelling folk, Holmes and I crept past. Rumblings of great anger could be heard, and one or two unfortunate costermongers were caught up in the vast swirling mob and found themselves suspended by the railings. The pair of us made our way through by stealth, occasionally breaking bottles over each other's heads and brandishing pictures of the Royal Family to assure passers-by that we belonged to the mob.

Scarce had we broken through the front ranks of the demonstrators, with Constable Hounslow movingly recounting that his foo was called Arthur and he tied the ends to look like a moustache, when a whoosh of fire from an upstairs bedroom could be clearly seen in the street. Grabbing my sleeve and making a bold run for dear life, such was the crowd's bloodthirsty mood, we broke past the ranks of the mob and raced for safety.

Inside the hotel, we gathered our persons and took several deep breaths. The atmosphere of blood and degraded mob justice was pervasive and cruel; and if Holmes is a stickler about one thing, it is that any element of cruel, pervasive mob justice in his cases should be organic and not from any outside source. Indeed, as he dusted the minute elements of prole from his exterior, I fancy I saw the sniffily curled lip of a detective discarding unwanted assistance.

Patrons looked to us, as the freshest arrivals on their scene, for some explanation of the bizarre, not to say frightening, scene that was taking place only feet from their teacups.

"Have no fear, ladies and gentlemen," Holmes began suavely. "It is true to say that the mob outside is brutal and bloodthirsty, that they shall not be content until blood is gushing down the street in great tidal waves, when your dead bodies are mangled and splattered and all exhibit the most frightful signs of violence."

A rippling sound of fear swept through the room, which curiously, sounded like everyone shitting themselves in rotation. Ever the dramatist, Holmes looked about him grimly, his worried eye flickering from face to uncomfortable face. Knowing him as well as I do, I could detect the glee with which his melodramatic soul was revelling in the moment.

"However," he continued, and at this juncture a small, well-dressed man tweaked Holmes' elbow and muttered into his ear, "I am told by the hotel manager here that, for as long as your safety is threatened by this swelling mass of brutal humanity just outside, boiled eggs are half price. Order now to avoid disappointment, especially as the lines of riot police may break at any moment, and you don't want to be dead before it arrives."

With these sage words ringing in their ears, the wealthy patrons went back to their newspapers, toast and gout. Order was restored about the place, and once again the serious matter of tackling crime was left to the experts. Or, in this case, us. Never mind. It's the younger generation I worry for.

As we headed for the stairs, I took a look back at the straining lines of riot cops. My eyes were met with scenes of thespian struggle which, for the good of all humanity, should never be recounted.

Without the merest courtesy of a knock, Holmes strode into the master bedroom in Freud's suite of rooms. For an instant he stopped as though transfixed, hands poised on the door handles and his whole figure so still as to be frozen.

From around his back I could see the scene of disarray. A considerable struggle had evidently taken place. There were items of clothing strewn about his randomly, as if tossed by a violent hand, and much of the furniture had been upset if not outright destroyed.

"Egad," I murmured, unprepared for these signs of destruction. "What manner of savage can have performed this outrage?"

An elderly figure walked into the room, clearly experiencing acute distress. Attending him was an devoutly observant figure, a young woman who ministered to him as if he were wealthy and about to make a will.

From the hysterical weeping of the man, I decided that he must have been a close relative of Dr Freud.

Clearly the young lady was his trophy wife or, if one does not rule out incest, a daughter hell bent on distracting him from his grief, and even going so far as to repeatedly squeeze his backside. When she did this, he tenderly patted her hand, as if thanking her for the thought, and then resumed his cries of woe.

Holmes and I waited for a moment as he composed himself, wondering if we were seeing some exotic continental grieving ritual. Eventually my colleague cleared his throat and took charge of the situation.

"Were you acquainted with Dr Freud?" Holmes asked, once more the commanding self of old. The man, evidently distraught, was not yet capable of speech. His young accomplice, clearly some angel faced temptress, was trying to ease his troubles by cooing sweetly to him about vast selling franchises and TV rights, whatever they might be.

The man evidently took some solace from her honeyed words and insistent stroking. He wiped some of his many tears on his hand and struggled for a moment to calm himself before speaking.

"We are ruined, Mr Holmes, ruined!" sobbed the man, who transpired to be Freud's publisher. He took a large cheque out of his pocket and blew his nose on it.

Holmes observed him with his characteristically languid hauteur.

"A bizarre reaction to a crime which may well leave a man's life in the balance," mused Holmes philosophically. "Would it be fair to say you were not on good terms with the deceased? I mean, the departed. That is to say, the missing."

The publisher looked at Holmes through strained eyes.

"He was our biggest seller, Mr Holmes. You've no idea how profitable are the realms of the furry bits are when you can call it science. Retiring and previously unblemished citizens have been exploring themselves, guilt free, in an unprecedented way! Now, refined old soldiers needn't shoot themselves whenever they have an erection. People are wearing leotards in public. They'll be finding the clitoris next!"

I could see from his reaction that Holmes was against this free thinking, no holds barred, get the old chap out and wave it under people's noses way of doing things. The publisher pressed on.

"You see, the thing is, I was coming round today with details of Dr Freud's next book. I was hoping that, having made it perfectly acceptable to think, fondle and even talk about our pleasure parts, he could do the same for bank robbery, incest and even murder!"

It was a pretty speech, but the only effect it had on my erstwhile companion was to make his eyebrows reach for the stratosphere.

"I see we have quite different motives for wanting to retrieve this man. I am motivated by a fixated, burning desire for justice to prevail, with her strong, lustful arms and big, throbbing tips, whereas you, in your apparel visibly stained by smutty vile pleasures, thinking of either money or a complete abandonment of moral standards. Quite a pretty piece of moral chicanery, I think you'll agree, eh, Watson?"

I 'umm'ed and 'oo'ed as expected, while noting the phrase "fixated, burning desire" in the notebook I keep specifically for writing in odd passing thoughts, such as "big, throbbing tips." The stain remark I would save for my special big, illustrated scrapbook of Holmes' nutty dribblings.

"Perhaps I have been too frank with you," said the publisher with a dismissive wave of his hand. The all too attentive lady took the cue and wiggled off, whereupon her employer turned to Holmes with a gesture that said plenty. Holmes' eyes briefly padoiinged from her shapely rear and did several laps back and forth around the room. They replanted themselves with a rattle and he struggled, with a sizeable gulp of air, to angle himself on top once more.

"A most interesting development," said he, coughing loudly in a vague attempt to regain his poise. "I'm not sure I can fully eliminate you from my enquiries. Perhaps a few questions. What were you doing at the time of the kidnapping?"

"I don't know, when was it?"

"A most reasonable question, and one to which the guilty party would certainly know the answer. It is my belief that you are both innocent of the crime, nor yet a witness, and still can answer that vital question. By merely writing down any hour of the day on a piece of paper, we can know for certain when this crime was committed!"

"Why Holmes, this is fantastical! I know you too well to doubt your methods, but what you suggest seems to me quite impossible."

Holmes was not deterred by my doubt; in fact, he was most positively heartened by it.

"My dear doctor, you don't think that I, too, as a man of science, recognise how that may seem to be an impossible proposition? But you forget Muntvarken's Final Law. If the situation of an experiment is altered, then the results may be different!"

"Stating the bloody obvious if you ask me, Holmes."

"Indeed. However I based my previous suggestion on the most fascinating research of the celebrated Norwegian doctor Alaheim Struu, who, you may

165

recollect, stunned the Nobel Academy. His Simple Principle is that when any number, time or date is guessed, if enough people write it down, scientifically speaking, one of us is bound to be right."

I paused for a moment to let this sink in.

"It's as good an idea as any we've got, I'm afraid. Perhaps we'd just better get on with it."

Holmes and I exchanged a meaningful glance, while from the outside we could hear the once rebellious crowd cooing softly to the strains of a strapping West Country copper intoning "Oi'm Constable Durham and oi loicke moi fuzzbox so much oi boight it a noice new ribbon."

Our silence was broken by the publisher clearing his throat in a meaningful way.

"I think perhaps I will not be able to offer you my assistance, Mr Holmes. This is a great shock to me, a terrible blow, and I need my solitude. Will you forgive me if I retire to my room? It is situated on the same floor as this. I shall be inconsolable for the rest of the day, seeing nobody apart from my assistant and only then for the purposes of accepting brief fellatio."

"Quite so. I think perhaps I shall fiddle obsessively with my pipe while you leave."

Gloomily raising my eyes heavenward at this scene, I could only voice my assent and brood on the matter for a quick moment. A sharp chime struck from deep within the inner bellows of my waistcoat. For a second I was dumbstruck, and then I remembered setting my fob watch alarm to remind Miss Bellamy about my evening nibble. It was with gladdened heart that I pulled out my Hunter and pushed in the little bell.

Holmes' eyes narrowed as he drank in the scene.

"You know, instead of merely guessing the time of the kidnapping, I have another idea."

I breathed a silent prayer of relief and surreptitiously dislodged a nut from my new loincloth. I was breaking in fresh underwear following recent criticisms of my faithful old Long Johns. These fine comfy articles had been replaced by a garishly coloured new leather ensemble, and I was finding the strain pretty terrific. Simply thinking about lunch shifted the pressure enough to twist my face into a purple mask of agony. Covering the thonk of my freed testicle with a discreet cough, I asked the great sleuth about his next move.

"I shall be questioning anyone at all who entered this suite, or who had other business with the doctor. If there is a clue to be found here, it lies with those who had access to the rooms. Mark you my words, Watson, it will be a trifling detail, the smallest break in routine, that catches our crook."

I agreed and called room service for witnesses, opting, for the sake of my professionalism, against ordering a great many sandwiches.

The first to arrive was a dapper, impeccably dressed old man. His smile was of sufficient brilliance to outshine a jeweller's window, and in his hand he carried an old, notched cane. Noting the continued symbolism of the narrative, I could only continue and silently hope no worse befell my nib.

He introduced himself to us with a firm, affectionate, even lustful handshake.

"It is my profoundest pleasure to meet you both, distinguished gentlemen of London's criminal elite. Pray tell me, purely for curiosity's sake, of course, how much does it cost to have a man killed these days?"

There was a brief hesitation as Holmes toyed with his ear and rolled his eyes about the place thoughtfully.

"I have heard one can obtain such services for as little ten shillings. That is, of course, should you not mind an ineffably messy, bungled job and the certainty of prison. However, for all your killing needs, may I strongly suggest you employ Derek the Pro, a sterling fellow with an unblemished reputation in the terminatory field. His rate is, I believe, five guineas a head, but it is piece of mind that your are buying. Here is his business card."

I must have been staring at Holmes aghast, for his eyes lit upon me with an inquisitive glance. He blustered for a second and then waved his hand dismissively before my eyes.

"Pah! I have a living to earn, Watson, and since my last four cases ended in death, litigation and a horsewhipping for an entirely innocent bailiff, the emergency telegrams bidding me to drop everything and save lives have been drying up. One eats where one can."

He turned back to the highly polished gent with the bemused expression in his keenly intelligent eyes.

"Good. I see you are a pair of slimy criminals. We know where we are. I congratulate you on this clarity."

"Only one slimy criminal," I retorted hotly, noting Holmes' hugely over-brilliantined hair with disapproval.

"Quite so," said the suave one. "However, you are investigating this matter, as I understand it, and I most particularly wish to do all in my power to help the enquiry."

"Who, pray, are you?"

"My full title is of no concern. I would be happy for you gentlemen to call me Alphonse."

"Indeed. Tell me, Alphonse, what is your connection with Dr Freud?"

The old man exhaled softly and tucked his thumbs into the sides of his waistcoat.

"It was in 1893, I believe, that I first met the doctor. I was enjoying myself in Vienna, dallying in a number of fashionable resorts. One day I was strolling down a street in the most delightful sunshine, enjoying the walk and eating a large and particularly phallic baguette. Such was his amusement at this implied virility in I, an old man with an inside leg of a sparse few inches, that he fell about laughing. We have been the best of friends ever since."

During this interesting speech Holmes had been musing quietly, his gaze flickering over the scene and that giant brain whirring away like the Dickens. What Holmes' brain was up to, I have no idea.

"As I see it, this crime is not a direct result of Dr Freud's activities. Would you agree with my assessment, Alphonse?"

"That depends upon your reading of the British mood and character, my good Holmes. If you consider the radical willy elements involved in psychoanalysis, it is not impossible, surely, to allow the hypothesis that an action group desirous of keeping an unhealthy air of mystique around their furry utensils of desire has acted? Such a group of people would have a very great deal to gain from Dr Freud's disappearance."

Holmes pursed his lips and eyed the room about him with fresh disapproval.

"There is much in what you say, Alphonse. However, we must not forget the individual. Do we not agree that Dr Freud is among the foremost practitioners in his field?"

"Without question, Mr Holmes. Before Dr Freud's breakthrough, most psychology was based on drinking piss and groping ducks."

Holmes nodded. Indeed, I, as a medical man, was familiar with the difficulties of treating patients with neuroses in the olden days. The duck shortage and absence of flavouring for piss made life difficult.

"Indeed," said Holmes, warming to his theme. "Is it not possible that Dr Freud may be testing the mettle of his devotees? He fakes his own kidnapping to draw out the best of his followers, perhaps leaving one or two key hints as to where he may be found. This achieved, he then retires to a safe distance from which to observe the events to follow." Holmes paused for a moment, and fixed us with a glittering eye. "Might this not be

169

plausible? A possible explanation of the matter to hand?"

I voiced my agreement gladly.

"A most sage analysis, old chap," I said, pleased to have been at hand for yet another astounding breakthrough. "I feel you have already unravelled much of the matter to hand. A couple of decent clues and then we can go back to Baker Street and puzzle the matter out. I can have a nap and you can do the rest of brainwork. Brilliant!" I felt so confident of Holmes' intuition that I reached into my pocket and made sure my patented sleeping goggles were close to hand.

Holmes looked as cheered as I, evidently having forgotten his own dictum about not leaping to conclusions. We spent the next several minutes looking around for psychological clues. Only Alphonse appeared agitated, even disheartened.

"Just as you say, gentlemen. It is not my view, but it is not my case, either. I leave it in your capable hands." With that he swept out regally, leaving the door to close behind him with an aloof click. I turned to Holmes with a smile.

"I fear you have offended him, Holmes."

My colleague smiled and became his elusive, enigmatic self again, and sank into deep thought. He looked around him slowly and deeply, an effusion of enlightenment elongating his features. I enjoyed the moment of silence, and took a moment to regret not having read past the e's in my thesaurus.

Several minutes of absorbed quiet allowed our thoughts to continue uninterrupted; Holmes' rigidly fixed on the crime, mine straying to both my sleeping goggles and Mrs Bellamy's new corset. My pleasant musings were interrupted by a slow, steady hiss. My nostrils quivered. I looked over to Holmes, and found his aquiline nasal features flexed and straining at the leash like a moored bull freshly kicked in the spuds.

"Treachery, Watson!" Holmes was poised for motion, his features thrown into the uproar of vital energy. "Shoot out all the windows!"

With an inward cry of revulsion, for I had seen victims of gas attacks, I drew my revolver, taking a moment to untangle my Mrs Bellamy's Thursday panties from the barrel.

Three shots cleared the main window over by the side dresser. Two more took out the ornamental carving of Big Ben on the mantelpiece and the sixth about twenty pounds' value out of the sideboard. Breathing heavily, Holmes staggered over to the main windows and, with slashing motions, used his umbrella to clear the frame.

For a moment only we breathed easily. Then a small, wizened figure in hotelier's uniform entered the room and started assessing the damage. Holmes, as revolted to the idea of financial outlay as myself, voiced his protest.

"I fear this is somewhat untoward, my good man. The inestimable Dr Watson, acting with a speed and resolution it is hard to over praise, and an aim difficult to worsen, saved our lives. Breathe lightly, sir! The vapours of poison gas may still be virulent within these chambers, and I fear for your aged lungs!"

"And I fear for your young brain, sir," replied the old git. "You may observe that the hissing sound of escaping gas is still audible. Also, please inhale sharply. You will, I think, detect the odour of cigars, knicker elastic and brandy; this is a custom perfume Herr Freud has made to his own exacting specifications. He brought it with him as it is, I gather, essential to his mental well being."

"I bet it is!" I agreed heartily, and wondered if said wonder-brew was available for general consumption.

We left the hotel under something of a cloud, with Holmes bullshitting furiously about being able to detect elements of poison with his ears and so forth. I don't think they believed it, but naturally were glad to see us go. No hotel of any quality likes guests shooting up the suites.

Our first port of call for enquiry was a celebrated institute of British mental health expertise; Happiness Equals Less Liberty. Holmes told me on the way he had a contact there, a most distinguished professor and lecturer.

We rapped on the door.

"Can I help you, sirs?" enquired a doddery retainer, sporting four more sizes of hat than was good for him.

"Yo homie-" began Holmes with a big inhalation of breath, spreading his fingers sideways in territorial proclamation. He gets these moments of odd mannerisms. I drew a discreet veil over his over-enthusiasm for puns with a swift elbow to the wind.

"We are here to speak with the mind wizard," I said, being familiar with modern medical parlance for those skilled in treating the mentally disadvantaged. It was, I am told, a good way to meet royalty.

"If you would step this way, gentlemen."

Pleased with this generous compliment, I trundled over the threshold. Holmes followed imperiously, looking especially snooty.

We followed him along a corridor lined with many rooms, from which emanated noises of foulest drooling. Bizarre raving shrieks wailed around distant corners ahead of us and my spirits shrank down into the heels of my socks.

"Holmes!" cried a voice somewhere amid a throng of savage looking loons with wild hair. "It is you, my dear fellow. Over here!"

Holmes grasped my arm to move with him as he hastened with all alacrity to the waving man.

"This," he whispered to me, "is the face of real psychology. Watson," he said, resuming his normal volume. "This is Professor Jack Barking, a colleague of mine from my alma mater. Barkers, meet Doctor James

172

Watson, my erstwhile friend, narrator and human shield."

The assembled inmates of this bizarre institution immediately backed away from us like we were gods among the damned, or as though Holmes had unleashed one of his sly onion specials.

If this unusual crowd reaction perturbed Holmes' friend, there was no sign amid his dauntless enthusiasm.

"Hello old fellow," he spoke with delight, reaching out to shake one of my buttocks. My natural reaction to this outrage – a squeak of bluster, the rocketing eyebrows and just a hint of excitement – must have attracted his gaze for, off my expression, he followed up his opening remark.

"You must forgive my eccentricities, Doctor Watson. These are the ways in which I reach beyond the confines of the acceptable. Nevertheless, we achieve some astounding results. To take an example, nobody here complains of depression."

Naturally I was stunned by this impressive claim, and took the opportunity to ask him how he achieved this.

"Very simple. If anyone complains of depression, I always recommend treating them with a stout stick rammed between the cheeks. As such, few people complain of depression. Except those who enjoy the cure, but they aren't really depressed."

Put like that, it was astounding this medical genius had not achieved acclaim beyond being the star attraction at our local loony bin.

After a brief pause in which he preened himself with visible oil, he continued discoursing on the varied aspects and achievements of his work.

"We also do important work on class here. In the next corridor we will find an experiment which I hope will afford you gentlemen some small amusement."

Following him to a better-lit tunnel, more like a maze of rooms, we saw a group of researchers busying themselves with a variety of impressive equipment. I was, for the first time, relieved by Dr Freud's absence.

"Observe. The meters are connected to each subject by a small interconnection of bassoon like instruments. See here, we can monitor each patients' progress."

Sure enough, on closer inspection the dials read all the way from 'very dead' on the dial all the way round to 'strapping healthy.' The arrow on all subjects indicated they were in the finest health.

"You will note, gentlemen, how scientific terminology has been eschewed in favour of more readily accepted gauges and stages of the Englishman's physical health."

Beyond the bank of meters was a series of cells, each airtight with a glass front, so that the specimens may be observed. It was here where I could also see the use of bassoon influenced utensil came to the fore, and indeed one well placed gust of wind along the apertures of those gleaming, knotty lines would cause havoc, not to mention wrong notes.

With an eager sense of professional curiosity, Holmes and I clustered around to the side of this experiment. He, magnifying glass in hand, was doing a speedy bit of quick detecting, clocking in a number of variant factors and other points of, undoubtedly, great and forceful significance.

I looked at the varied range of men in the cells, some wearing tattered and stained overalls, others clad in what appeared to be the finest tailoring.

A very bizarre, even unique testing field, I found myself thinking.

The testing began as Professor Barking reached into his coat, produced a baton and flourished it. Various workers raced to a series of pumps over by the wall and began working their mechanisms.

Near instantly a gas began entering the chambers. The men began looking around them, some with great fear in their aspects, others looking around with mild curiosity as though a waiter were walking past with items of no great importance.

Scarcely a minute later, the health gauges on some of the specimens began wavering. Most hovered around 'cheerfully whistling,' then the needles on some began dropping quickly, to 'strapping healthy' then 'off work' before plummeting to 'I can't even make it to the pub,' and finally 'it's my back.'

These fellows were now clutching at their throats and looking decidedly below par. Curiously, it was only the fellows who were shoddily clad that had been affected. Those from the higher echelons of society, with their impeccable tailoring, were unperturbed.

"That was a mild nerve agent," said the genial professor, once he had called for the pumps to be closed and the gas desisted. "Prolonged exposure results in a variety of unpleasant side effects, one of which is death. Very sad. Although," he hastened to reassure us, "nobody has received a fatal dose."

Holmes and I brightened considerably and made our way over to the side of the glass chambers and began studying.

"As you gentlemen can see, the lower class people are struggling mightily. All are fighting for breath and some look as if they are close to death. Just so. Here, though, we see a rather different reaction."

The professor ambled over to the later cases, where the better-clad specimens were eyeing him with the unwelcoming hauteur of a dowager greeting a tramp come to woo her daughter.

Barking opened the vent, which allowed the men to speak.

"Oh I say, what a terrible whiff," was one of the first comments I heard, and indeed the upper crust chappies appeared to be mildly perturbed, at worst, by the experience. One fellow complained of having missed a round of golf and lunch at Buxella's for nothing, but then rather sportingly vouched that it was worth it to "help out an egghead."

"As you can see, the aristocrat – typically with one or more gold coronets in the family chest – has felt little or no problem at all with the nerve agent, which attacks one's feelings of social inferiority. The lower class fellows, on the other hand, have had a most distressing time of things. They would no doubt sue us if this were some feeble blame culture."

Stretchers arrived for the working class, who were carried away, griping feebly. The doors merely had to be opened for the better element, who left with graceful alacrity, adjusting their cuffs and screwing monocles into place as they left.

"Same time tomorrow, Sir Clarence?" asked Professor Barking of one of these men, giving him a sovereign as he spoke. The man took it with an aloof expression before thoughtfully pocketing the coin.

Very useful, these impoverished aristocrats.

Holmes viewed the scene with a clinical eye, the glint of approval shining through his stern features.

"A most interesting piece of science, Barkers. What is it that you are trying to achieve here?"

Professor Barking took his glasses off and polished them thoughtfully on his shirtsleeve before he answered.

"We are attempting to prove, beyond any shadow of doubt, that lack of nobility is killing England. I should point out, at this juncture, that our facility receiving a whopping grant and a royal warrant has absolutely no bearing on our work."

He leaned forward with a conspiratorial manner, and spoke in a breathy undertone.

"To be perfectly truthful, we only gave the working class people any poison. The other just smelt a particularly mild eau de cologne, scented with peppermint to make the whole thing convincing."

"Oh, that's all right then," we both said in relief.

"Now, before I forget, Sherlock, what was it you wanted to ask me?"

Holmes struck his forehead and then resumed his habitually cold professional manner.

"I must ask you, Professor Barking, was it you who kidnapped noted Austrian dream boffin Sigmund Freud?"

"No. Anything else?"

"No. Shan't take any more of your time, Barkers."

I raised my hat to the good professor and his staff. Holmes and I made our way out quietly, not wishing to disturb any other experimentation going on purely in the interests of science and humanity.

Upon returning to Baker Street, Holmes immediately sank into our deepest armchair and knitted his fingers firmly into a rest, onto which he placed his head. From this position I knew he would continue with his thoughts for days, even weeks, requiring only tobacco and a small bucket.

On the second day of his vigil of thought, during which he had stirred scarce at all, a telegram arrived from Scotland Yard. It was from one of Lestrade's subordinates, who begged us to race immediately to Dr Freud's last known address.

As such, we found ourselves revisiting the scene of the crime. The hotelier giving us a look of undisguised contempt.

Inspector Lestrade stood motionless, his eyes wide in shock. An expression of intense surprise was deeply engraved in his features. His eyes were large as billiard balls and empty in wonderment; his only movement an intense quivering of the lower lip, that wobbled with such regularity one could have used him for a cigarette rolling machine.

"Most curious," I said, observing the stricken inspector's state of statuesque rigidity and sticking a pencil up his nose. "It would appear that our friend

Lestrade has seen more than his burly policeman's brain can stomach."

Pausing to pull an odd expression at my last comment, Holmes pursed his lips and faced me.

"A somewhat confused metaphor, Watson, but I share your findings. Whatever the inspector saw was obviously a far greater strain than his feeble police issue marbles could handle."

Holmes reached for his shoulder holster and whipped out his extra large magnifying glass. The inspector's stricken visage was all the more terrible in exaggeration. Running his gaze over the stunned copper, Holmes noticed a volume at his feet, the cause, we both immediately surmised, of the inspector's current predicament.

The leather-bound book was lying on the floor, its pages still open. It was of the kind used by a manifold variety of professionals. Holmes stooped and retrieved this, his eyes flickering back and forth, bulging more and more as he absorbed the notebook's contents. As his expression of incredulity grew, I became more anxious to share in its contents. I tugged at Holmes' sleeve to share in his voyeurism.

"Ah! I see you have found Doctor Freud's notebook."

There was no answer, and indeed my good friend stood rooted to the spot, motionless in every manner. I contemplated dropping his trousers and then calling for the maid, just to see the reaction, but before I could do so a voice from behind caught my attention.

At this Holmes started back to life, and we both turned to face the speaker. We found a small gentleman addressing us. He had an exquisitely tiny head, shiny and pristine, and an almost gnome like expression. He regarded us with quizzical distance in his eyes, through a pair of pince-nez spectacles balanced precariously on his long nose.

"From reading the above, I see you are the narrator," he said, addressing me with an air of quiet congratulation which I felt he did not quite feel. I resolved to pat him very quickly on the head and kick him in the arse as soon as I could.

"I am sorry if you are displeased with what I said," he offered, reading the above sadly, the corners of his mouth turning down. "However, if you are looking for Doctor Freud's whereabouts, I think I may be able to help you."

Mightily heartened by his fine words, I turned to Holmes with delight. Before I could voice my exhilaration, I was struck at Holmes' expression which, for the first time in our long association, wore an expression of guilty shock.

"Ah yes, I am very glad to hear that," said he to our short shiny visitor. "Perhaps you should wait for a moment before continuing, as I need to very quickly think of a reason to get Doctor Watson out of the way."

"I fear I will not be able to oblige you, sir, as I am required across town in but one quarter of an hour, as my services are needed elsewhere. A rich family hire me as an occasional table," he said by way of explanation.

"If you will follow me downstairs, though, I do believe I can throw some light on the matter at hand. Please take this."

It was a receipt for parcel post, first class to Vienna. It even especially stipulated that under no circumstances should the air holes be covered, and that nitwit proof restraints should be used upon arriving.

"Apparently the parcel was returned to sender. It appears that it never even left London, as some prize beetroot brain forgot to include a return address. As you can see at the bottom, however, we see quite a distinct signature."

"Holmes!" I cried, aghast at the realisation of what my friend had done. "Do you mean to say you – you! I mean, you, of all people, arranged for the good doctor to disappear. All to save yourself from dissolving into a dissipated haze of boner-fuelled mayhem whenever certain issues arose in your devout bachelor's mind?"

Holmes bridled somewhat, then regained his composure.

"Certainly not, Watson. I fear you underestimate our Victorian populace and the levels of humanity it is prepared to embrace. This sexual pleasure you so readily fancy to be a human right is a mere frippery, and a distraction from the Englishman's true and traditional pleasures – those of drinking tea, social aspiration and quiet self loathing. I feel sure you will agree with me, when you are next at yourself and have ditched those most ridiculous Hawaiian shirts, that deviation from such tried and tested rituals would be mere folly."

He gazed at me for a moment, and in that long second I realised the truth of his words. For in every English born heart lives a desire for the simple, unexciting things in life. I reached into my pocket with a heavy, regretful hand. I tried to find my balls and my gun went off once again.

"I have this dream ... I'm naked and there's a giant magnifying glass chasing me ..."

"So it's a book, four words ..."

About The Author

Chris Wood is one of England's least distinguished writers, with pieces in some highly obscure publications and also *The Guardian*. Chris is proud of not having won the Booker prize three years in a row. Spike Milligan once told him to fuck off.

He is also the author of two writing guides, *The Ingredients Of A Good Thriller*, out now, and *The Ingredients Of A Good Horror*, due Summer 2009.

The Ingredients Of A Good Thriller

Ever wanted to write a thriller?

Ever thought you had a story but didn't know where to start?

This book gives you:

- A detailed breakdown of characters.
- Tips on getting the reader's attention.
- Ways of effectively telling stories.
- The impact of good dialogue.
- Explorations of top thrillers.
- Hints on how to give your story impact.

The Ingredients Of A Good Thriller is a guide to an area that has huge potential and gives great pleasure. It's an easy to follow approach to writing and improving your story. It provides solid examples to show you what works - and what doesn't.

Clear and easy to follow, this book is helpful for any thriller writer. Don't start without it!

Out now from LDB Publishing.

The Ingredients Of A Good Horror

Horror is always popular, and the last ten years have only seen an increase in this permanent favourite. Most people love ghost stories, tales of the supernatural and matters of murder.

If you're writing in this area, or are just interested, *The Ingredients Of A Good Horror* is for you.

This book looks at a wide variety of myths, superstitions, maniacs, curses, ghouls, monsters and ghosts. Easy to follow and full of useful information, this book breaks down the conventions of these stories in an entertaining and accessible way.

Imaginary creatures of the dark are discussed alongside real life nightmares, and the genre is considered in a way that appeals to writers and fans alike.

Coming Summer 2009 from LDB Publishing.

CPSIA information can be obtained at www.ICGtesting.com
Printed in the USA
LVOW081440080313

323402LV00006B/663/P